Lord of Pirates

BY
SCARLETT SCOTT

Lord of Pirates

When a dangerous-looking stranger raps on Lizzie Winstead's door in the middle of a stormy night, the peace of her humdrum life is shattered. She's shocked to discover her visitor is Captain Edmond Grey, one of the most feared pirates of the realm and her lost love.

Edmond is a wanted man throughout the Colonies, but despite his formidable reputation, he desperately needs help to nurse his wounded brother back to health. Only Lizzie can be trusted not to turn Edmond over to authorities for the price on his head.

Lizzie can't quell the feelings Edmond stirs in her heart or the fire he ignites in her blood. Before long, both succumb to the reckless desire renewed between them. She follows him aboard his pirate ship and sets sail into a world rife with passion and peril.

Together they brave fierce battles and frightening storms, determined to discover whether the love they once shared is strong enough to reunite them forever and conquer the demons of Edmond's past.

*Note: Originally published in *Wicked Rogue of Mine* collection August 2018, this is an extended version, never before published.*

Prologue

London, 1709

*L*IZZIE'S HAND WENT to the latch of the servant's entrance. She knew she was not meant to answer it, but someone had knocked, and with most of the household staff otherwise occupied preparing for the evening's festivities, she did not mind performing the easy task. They were expecting a cake delivery, as she well knew, and with many distinguished guests joining them tonight—including some of Father's esteemed physician colleagues—she did not dare ignore the caller.

She opened the door.

And promptly forgot about cakes, propriety, and the dinner that had the entire household in such a flurry. Forgot about everything. Everyone. Forgot to even breathe as she fell into the spell of a glittering, dark gaze.

Thump, thump, thump went her heart. It was a moment unlike any other, where she felt such a visceral connection to the young man before her, an utter stranger. She felt almost as if she knew him. As if he was somehow hers in an elemental way. Awareness flared deep within her, a tingling sensation tugging at her belly.

He felt it too.

She could sense it in the way he stood, unmoving as a marble bust, his gaze burning into hers. Here was someone who called to her, to a part of her she could not explain and had not even known existed until now. Until this handsome young gentleman in simple dress had appeared on the other side of the door and everything had changed.

"I have a delivery for your master, miss," he said, breaking the silence with a deep and soothing voice.

He had mistaken her for a servant, and for a beat, she did not wish to disabuse him of his conclusion, for fear it would change his easy manner with her. As the daughter of an eminent London physician, she was accustomed to tradesmen and domestics treating her differently. She was grateful to be Father's daughter, for the opportunity it afforded her to study his books alongside him as he permitted. But she did not like the unwritten difference between herself and others.

She was Lizzie Crawley, a simple young woman who loved to read and tend her herb garden. She was no one special.

"A delivery," she repeated slowly, her heart hammering ever faster. What was it about this stranger that made her pulse leap and her body awaken as if from a long slumber?

She did not know. Could not say. All she did know was that she could gaze upon him forever. He had a strong jaw, a firm chin bearing a small divot, a proud nose, slashing cheekbones, and his mouth…she could not help but wonder, in most shocking and inappropriate fashion, how that sinful mouth would feel against hers.

"Aye, miss." A subtle grin quirked his lips, as if he sensed the wayward direction of her thoughts. "I come from the baker, Allen and Son."

That would be the cakes she had ordered on Father's behalf. He was a learned man, content to study his books and practice medicine. Social matters were not of interest to him. This evening's dinner had fallen to Lizzie, in the place of her mother.

But this was not the baker she had met with three days prior. This young man was not short and stout, nor round-cheeked with eyebrows that resembled caterpillars. Nor did he smell of flour and grease. She took a discreet sniff of the air.

No. This man smelled of soap. Clean and tart and masculine.

"Of course," she forced herself to say, smiling as if her entire world had not just been upended by his appearance. "Forgive me. I was not expecting the delivery this early."

Why, before he had knocked, her day had been ordinary. She had been counting plates and making certain Father would be proud of her as his hostess this evening. She had been humming to herself, thinking the sunlight trickling through the windows surprisingly bright for an early spring day.

Was he the baker's son? When could she see him again, and how? Perhaps Father could host another dinner? Certainly ordering more cakes would not be too dear an expense. Cook possessed tolerable culinary prowess, but her desserts were undeniably dreadful. Hence the cakes. Hence the young gentleman who had not yet moved. The man who returned her stare with one of his own—assessing, searching, admiring.

He was intrigued, unless she missed her guess. That made two of them, for she was decidedly flummoxed. And hopelessly, helplessly drawn to him.

"I shall retrieve them and bring them in," he said, flashing her a smile that took her breath.

The smile was gone before she could react, and so was he, turning and disappearing toward the street with its bustling activity—carriages, tack, London going about its toil. How had she failed to notice the sound? How had she failed to notice a cloud had displaced the sun she'd been so admiring and that a gentle rain had begun to fall?

She watched him striding away, eyes devouring his tall, lean form. Beneath the hat he wore, his hair, long and dark, descended down his back from a queue at his nape. No wig for him, and she was thankful for it.

Thankful too for the sight of him returning, bearing the assortment of small cakes in his arms. She stepped back, allowing him entrance, and felt suddenly as if the chamber he had just entered was too small. He seemed to inhabit all of it with his presence.

"Where would you have me place them, miss?" he asked, showing not a hint of strain for his burden.

"Here, if you please," she said, gesturing to an empty space of table.

As she watched him lower the cakes to the beeswax-polished wood, she hoped quite fervently that none of the servants would return and interrupt them. She was enjoying herself far too much. She wanted him all to herself. And neither did she wish for anyone to return and inform him she was, in fact, the master's daughter rather than a maid in his employ.

He turned back to her, his gaze unreadable. "There you are, miss."

To her dismay, he walked back to the door, preparing to leave. Of course he would, she told herself, for he had likely been tasked with all manner of deliveries across town. He was performing his duty, whilst she was mooning over him, and she now realized he had not been affected at all. Likely, she had been wrong to think they shared a connection, to think the flicker of something between them had been more than a mere meeting of two strangers engaged in going about their respective days.

But he stopped at the last moment, turning back to her. "I have not seen you here before, miss."

"Do you always deliver the goods from the bakery?" she asked without answering, for she did not wish to dissemble.

A rueful grin curved his lips. "Aye, miss. For the nonce, just until Mr. Allen's new apprentice begins."

"Perhaps I shall see you next week," she said before she could stay the words. In private, her mind was whirling with the means by which she could convince Father to order more cakes, more buns, more confections of any sort. Anything to see him again. She had to know his name. "What are you called, sir?"

"Edmond Grey, miss." He touched two fingers to the brim of his hat. "Good day to you."

And then, he was gone.

Lizzie vowed she would see him again.

Two months later

EDMOND KNEW HE damn well didn't want to be a baker. Apprenticed from the time he was but a lad, he'd grown weary of flour, of baking buns, of never leaving the tedious life of shopkeeper. He'd finally settled upon the path that would lead him far away.

There was only one snag in the fabric of his otherwise flawless plan, and it was a large snag indeed.

Miss Elizabeth Crawley.

Lizzie, as he had come to know her.

He'd been wooing her in secret from the moment he'd delivered cakes to her father's home. He had been enamored from the first, for she was the loveliest girl he'd ever seen with golden hair and eyes the color of the summer sky. There had been an understanding between them—a deep, powerful bond—that had been instant and undeniable. He had fallen into her gaze that first day, and he had never been the same.

Initially, he had believed her a servant, and she had not corrected him. If he had known she was the daughter of a physician—a lady far above the likes of him, he would never have pursued her. Indeed, he would not have returned with the next delivery or the next. Nor would he have kissed her or held her in his arms, even if the notion of never having kissed her filled his chest with a hollow ache.

Because she was not meant to be his, and she had never been meant to be his. He had never possessed any intention of becoming a baker. For all his life, he had dreamt of the water. When he had been sleeping and dreaming, awake and wishing he was asleep, whenever his mind wandered, the restless yearning returned. He wanted freedom. He longed for the call of the ocean and a boat listing beneath his feet. He could not bear to remain, to settle into his life as a baker, toiling day and night to earn a livable wage whilst hating himself.

And so, here he stood, hesitating at the gate that separated him from her. When he walked through, it would be as the man who loved her. But when he passed back through, it would be as the man who was leaving her. For he had no choice other than to tell her goodbye.

He found her in the herb garden she so diligently kept. She didn't hear him approach, and he allowed himself a moment's pause to admire her for the last time. Her blonde hair had been plaited into a fat braid and she wore an old mantua stained with mud, but she was still the most gorgeous creature he'd ever seen.

"Lizzie."

She spun about, holding a hand to her breast. "Good heavens, Edmond. You startled me."

"Pray forgive me." He crossed the distance between them,

feeling like the worst sort of cad for what he must do. He didn't want to hurt her. Hurting her would be akin to carving one of his own organs from his body. But he had no choice. The path before him was not meant for a soft, gentle lady like Lizzie. She was too kind, too sweet, and he would not be the source of her bitterness or ruination.

"Of course." She smiled, wiping at the smears of dirt upon her dress. "You must forgive me for my appearance."

"You are lovely as ever." Edmond caught her hands in his, not caring that they were encrusted in dirt from her ministrations. He took a deep breath, held it in his lungs for a beat longer than necessary, before expelling the air and the beginning of their inevitable end. "It is I who needs the ultimate absolution."

Her blue gaze searched his, questioning. "Why do you say that?"

He plowed ahead, knowing there was no kind way to break ties with her. "Lizzie, I'm leaving."

She smiled, cocking her head at him as if puzzled. "Must you be off already? You've only just arrived."

Her innocence stabbed at his heart. "No, love. I've joined the navy."

Her eyes flared. "The navy?"

He nodded. "I'll be leaving on a ship in the morning."

"I see." Her expression became cautious, her brow furrowed as she attempted to digest his revelation. "When will you be returning?"

And here it was, the part that felt like a knife sinking into his heart. He stared at her sweet round face, her ethereal loveliness, his gaze dipping to the fullness of her pink lips for one more longing look. If he gazed upon her long enough, hard enough, it seemed to him that he could commit her face to his memory forever. That he could take this small sliver of her along with him, the only part of her he would allow himself to keep.

Say it, Edmond.

Tell her, you bloody coward.

She waited, so trusting, heart on her sleeve.

He severed the final tie binding them together, surging forward as he knew he must. One day, she would thank him. One day, she would find a man worthy of her love. And he hated that nameless, faceless man with the rancor of a thousand stinging suns.

"Edmond?" She had begun to pale, her eyes searching his, comprehension dawning.

"I won't be," he rasped.

"Not returning." The warmth bled from her voice, the welcome from her face. She looked stricken. "Never?"

He released her hands and brushed a stray tendril of hair from her cheek. "I don't belong here."

She flinched away from his touch. "You don't belong here? How dare you court me and lead me to believe you harbored tender feelings for me? What was I to you? A lark?"

Guilt skewered him. In truth, he'd fallen in love with Lizzie. He'd never wanted to cause her pain. For a time, he had thought he could fashion himself into the man she deserved, but each day he served in the bakery stole another piece of his soul. One day, there would be nothing left, and he would resent the wife who had tied him to a trade he deplored. London was not for him. A quiet life was not his idea of happiness. He was hungry for adventure, travel. The sea called.

He checked the urge to reach for her again, for he had forfeited that right. Still, he would not have her believe he had not cared for her. "Of course not, Lizzie. You were never anything less than everything to me. But the truth is that I would sooner swallow poison than spend the rest of my life as a baker. I have to leave, find my own fortune rather than the one my father chose for me."

She studied him in that way she had, seeming to see straight through him. "You have made this decision because of your father."

Edmond despised Sir John Grey. He made no secret of the sad fact, nor did he make any apologies. Indeed, for the majority of his eight and ten years, he'd done his best to ignore his sire's existence.

He was one of two brothers, both born bastards. His mother was an utter saint, and she'd done her utmost to raise Edmond and Thomas as proper young men. Sir John was a fine gentleman who had no wish to be saddled with the illegitimate get produced by his youthful follies. He used his influence to obtain apprenticeships for Edmond and Thomas both and had only bothered to meet them on one occasion. Edmond had always been brutally honest with Lizzie about the truth of his lineage.

Yes, he supposed his father had a great deal to do with his decision. One day he would prove to Sir John Grey he was a man worthy of respect. "I need to make my way, Lizzie. This is my choice."

"There will be no changing your mind, will there?" She was quiet.

He did his damnedest to ignore the sheen in her eyes. Her calm acceptance nearly undid him, and every part of him longed to sweep her back into his arms where she belonged, to kiss her luscious lips and promise her that he would find a way back to her.

But he could not.

He was not for her, he told himself. He was doing both of them a favor. "It's far better for me to leave you now than to roam from you after we're wed," he forced himself to say, though he knew it in his heart as a lie. If Lizzie Crawley were his, he would have never left her side. It was why he needed to leave now. "Please understand."

"I don't think I ever shall." She rose on tiptoe to press a kiss to his cheek, the peck burning into his skin like a brand. "I wish you well, Edmond. Know that wherever you go I will always hold you in my heart and prayers." Tears streamed unabashedly down her soft skin.

"Thank you." Hell and damnation, this was difficult. Leaving her was not easy, and he hated himself for having to do it. In the end, he knew one day she'd thank him. She deserved to be loved by a true man, not by a bastard who was filled with the hunger to rove the seas. "I will never forget you, Lizzie."

"Nor I you," she whispered.

And then he left her to her herb garden and a life without him. As Edmond walked away, a fine mist began to fall. He'd never felt more like a bastard than he did in that moment.

Chapter One

Philadelphia 1719

$\mathcal{A}$T FIRST LISTEN, Lizzie mistook the commotion for thunder from the angry spring rainstorm that had been assaulting the city since sundown. She stilled at her writing desk, pen poised above the notes she'd been transcribing on one of her father's medical treatises. No indeed, the loud pounding sound was not caused by a storm, she realized with growing concern, but someone at the front door.

She dropped her pen in its inkwell and stood. Only a desperate person would call at the house of a physician at this hour, someone in dire need of aid. With her father gone to Boston to visit with an old associate from London, Lizzie would have to see to the patient as best she could. Although she had not been permitted to attend university, she had served as her father's apprentice for nearly half her twenty-eight years. She only hoped the problem was one with which she was already familiar. After all, she was unaccustomed to practicing on her own.

The knocking grew in intensity. There was no time to tarry. She secured the wrapper she'd donned over her night shift. Although she was hardly dressed to receive a visitor, she had little choice. Taking a candle with her, she left her bedchamber and navigated her way downstairs.

By the time she reached the front hall, the ever-efficient

Jeremiah and Judith, her father's faithful retainers, waited.

"Shall I answer, Mrs. Winstead?" Jeremiah asked in grim tones.

Philadelphia was still relatively young and could, at times, be quite rough. However, Lizzie could never deny care to someone in need on account of a misplaced sense of caution. Indeed, her father had asked her to carry on in his absence should the need arise.

Praying it was not some drunkard or scoundrel at their door, she nodded to Jeremiah. "Please do, Jeremiah. I'm certain it must be one of Papa's patients."

"Yes, madam." Raising his candle high, he swung open the front door to reveal a large silhouette.

"I need to see Dr. Crawley at once," announced their guest in a voice as low as it was commanding.

"He's not at home," Jeremiah responded. "Can I help you in some way, sir?"

"Rouse him from bed if you must. Damn my blood, I don't have time for a servant with a cane up his arse."

Irritated at the man's rudeness, Lizzie swept forward. Jeremiah was of slight build with graying hair and a gouty limp. If their unexpected guest wanted to cause trouble, he easily could. Best to try to tamp down a problem before it began.

"I'm afraid my father is out of town, sir." She tried to peer through the murkiness of the night to see the man's face but could discern only long hair too straight to be a wig. The brim of his hat hid all else from her view.

"Lizzie?" Disbelief underscored the stranger's tone.

Something about that rough, demanding voice sent a trill down her spine. A trigger of remembrance flared in her stomach. His use of her father's pet name for her more than startled her. She could not shake the sense that she knew this man.

But how and who?

She stiffened. "Sir, do I know you?"

"Indeed." Silence descended for a beat, interrupted only by the slashing rain and violent rumble of the storm beyond him. "I'm an old family…friend. Might I have a private word with you?"

When she hesitated, he spoke again, cajoling. "I beg of you, Lizzie. It is a matter of life and death."

He spoke like a gentleman but hardly looked like one even in the dim light. That he would not reveal himself before the servants was particularly telling. Her instincts told her to shut the door in his face, bar it, and never think of him again. But there was an urgency in his tone, a pleading almost. Her heart was ever too soft.

"You may come inside," she conceded after a long pause. "Judith, please put on a pot of water for tea."

"Mrs. Winstead," Jeremiah protested, giving voice to her private concerns.

"Our guest is a family friend, Jeremiah. Please stand by should we need you." She would give the man the privacy he requested, but not the opportunity to do mischief. If Jeremiah remained within earshot, she would feel somewhat safe, at least. She inclined her head to the mysterious man before her. "Follow me, sir."

Lizzie led him into her father's study and lit a handful of tapers. The light afforded her the opportunity to make a closer inspection of the man. He wore a greatcoat over the customary fearnothing jacket of seamen, and a pair of breeches and boots much finer than the rest of his garments. He appeared thoroughly sodden from the rains. His hair was dark, perhaps black, his features mostly obscured by a beard. He looked, in fact, like a man who was dangerous.

She placed her candle on her father's desk and clasped her hands at her waist, trying to staunch the unease sliding through her. "Pray explain who you are, sir, and what brings you to our door at this time of night."

"First, I must have your word that what I tell you remains between us only."

Lizzie scoffed. "I hardly think you're in a position to make demands of me."

In two strides he closed the distance between them. His large hands clamped on her waist, which was nearly naked without her customary stays and stomacher. She felt the heat of him through the thin fabric as the salty scent of sea water assailed her. He yanked her flush against his body.

Excitement mingled with fear as he held her. It had been years since a man had touched her so intimately and she was shocked to discover a stranger could have such an effect upon her.

"Listen closely, Lizzie. You've a gouty old man and woman for protection and nothing else. I haven't the time to play bloody games with you. I'll have your promise or you'll pay the price," he growled.

Beneath the commanding boom of his voice hid a lingering sense of familiarity. Comprehension hit her with the force of a runaway stallion. She knew the man before her. Hand shaking, she reached up and traced the strong edge of his jaw. The bristles of his beard tickled her fingertips. She studied his eyes, his sensual full mouth. He had changed much, but beneath the grizzled façade of a seaman she recognized the first man she'd ever loved.

"Edmond," she whispered. "Can it be? Is it you?"

"I'll have your promise, damn you," he insisted, giving her a soft shake.

"I promise." She said it with ease, knowing now why he'd

been so secretive, so distressed.

The suitor of her youth had run off to the navy and in-stead of pursuing an honorable career, he'd become one of the most feared pirates in the realm. Captain Edmond Grey's exploits were legendary. He was a wanted man, the Scourge of the Atlantic. If anyone learned of his presence on shore, he'd be arrested or murdered on sight. Just the year before, the infamous pirate Blackbeard had been killed in Virginia, his severed head hung from a ship's bowsprit as warning to all who presumed to follow in his path.

"I'm entrusting you with my life, Liz—Mrs. Winstead." He paused. "Where is your husband?"

He had taken careful note, then, of Jeremiah's form of address. Sadness swept over her. Her hand stilled at Edmond's chin. She had loved her husband, but never as she'd loved the wild man before her. A decade had gone by since he had walked from her life, and yet a day hadn't passed that she had not thought of him, of what might have been.

But she must not allow her feelings for the suitor she had once known to impede her decisions now. The past was where it belonged, and that old Edmond Grey had been replaced by she knew not what manner of savage.

"Your husband," Edmond pressed, an edge to his voice. "Where is he?"

She blinked, returning to the present. To this bleak night and the storm and the ghost from her past it had somehow resurrected. "He passed on five years ago."

He swallowed. "Hell, I'm sorry to hear it. I'm sure he was a good man."

"He was, thank you." She forced a small smile to her lips. "He has gone on to a greater reward. Now tell me, Captain Grey. What has brought you here? Have you any idea how much danger you've put yourself in?"

"Of course I know." His grip on her waist tightened. "I wouldn't be here unless it was necessary. I need a physician, Mrs. Winstead. We ran into a skirmish with a navy frigate. The *Freedom* is faster and we outran them, but our casualties were heavy. Our ship's surgeon was killed, many others wounded." He stopped, his voice breaking. "My brother Thomas among them."

The physician's daughter in her suddenly took precedence over the woman who had once loved the man before her. Or at least the young man she'd thought him to be. This dark, bearded stranger, so much taller and broader than he'd been in his youth, was unknown to her. A criminal. A man she dared not trust.

"How bad is it?" she forced herself to ask.

"Very bad." He set her away from him and turned to pace the length of the room. "He took a musket ball to the head."

Lizzie gasped. "He is still alive?" It was almost unheard of for any man to survive an injury to the head.

"He is breathing, yes. I haven't any idea how bad it is. I'm afraid…damn my blood, I'm afraid he's going to die. It's all my fault. I should have bloody well told him no when he asked to come away with me. I knew the risks I was taking and I didn't give a damn. I shouldn't have allowed it." With a cry, he slammed his fist into the wall.

Her heart gave a pang at his raw grief. Hesitant to intrude upon his anguish, she approached him slowly and placed a hand on his coat. "You must not blame yourself. It was Thomas' choice to follow you."

A knock at the door interrupted them. Judith entered at Lizzie's request, bearing a tray of tea. Lizzie smiled to reassure the concerned maid. "Place it on the desk, if you please, Judith. You may go, thank you."

Lizzie turned to the tea service, dear to have in the Colonies, and fixed two steaming cups, finding comfort in the familiarity of the routine. Edmond's presence and his revelations had shocked her.

She offered a cup to Edmond, hand shaking. "You look as if you could use warming."

He let out a bark of bitter laughter. "I prefer rum, my dear Mrs. Winstead. I have mere hours to find a physician for my brother before my ship returns for me."

Mrs. Winstead. Although it was a name she had answered to for years, hearing it uttered in his low, gruff rumble felt odd. She blinked, dispelling the errant realization. *This man is a stranger to you, Lizzie. You cannot trust him or allow your past association with him to cloud your judgment.*

What had he wanted? *Ah, yes. Rum.* She gave him her most disapproving frown. "I'm afraid we haven't any spirits, sir. Besides, tea is far better for the constitution."

Edmond accepted the cup, his dark-brown gaze searching hers. "You sound like my sainted mother."

Lizzie bowed her head, peering into the contents of her tea as if it would provide her the answers she sought. "I am no one's mother."

If only she could have repressed the twin threads of sadness and regret in her voice. Many times she had wished she'd been able to conceive with her husband. Having a child would have made her loneliness more bearable. She had Father, of course, but each year that passed left her increasingly aware that one day, she would be alone in the world. Even if she married again, her childless marriage to Richard suggested she was barren.

"I'm sorry, damn it." Edmond took a draw of the tea, bringing her focus back to him. "I haven't been in polite society in years. I'm not fit company for a lady like you."

"You haven't thrown me over your shoulder and carried

me away to your ship yet." She hoped her attempt at levity would lighten their conversation and steer them into safer subjects. Subjects that did not involve the past and her ocean of regrets.

Instead, his gaze darkened as it roamed slowly over her body. She became aware of how few layers of fabric separated her from him. Two to be precise. Edmond Grey was frighteningly handsome and looking at her in the way a man had not looked upon her in some time. A rush of warmth pooled between her thighs, and her cheeks went hot.

"Not yet." Warning darkened his words, serving as a reminder this was no social call. Captain Grey was no lovesick suitor from her youth, returned to woo and win her. He was a lawless ruffian.

She ought to fear him and the depravities it was said he'd committed in his treasonous plundering of the seas. Instead, her feelings for him, despite the intervening years, had never altered. They thrummed within her now like a steady ache.

Her initial anger, fierce and painful as a blade, had dissipated over the years, leaving sadness in its wake. After time had gone by, she'd recognized the struggle he must have faced, trying to make his own mark on the world, not wanting to hurt her. The girl she'd once been saw before her not the feared pirate he had become but the charming young man she had known.

Part of her longed to comfort him, take him in her arms. She physically ached with how much she'd missed him. As she'd promised, she'd never forgotten. She'd loved her husband, but she had not forgotten Edmond Grey.

Best to quell such troublesome thoughts, she decided. She should be worrying more about how to best help his wounded brother and less about unrequited emotions for an outlaw. There could be no future between a respectable widow and a pirate, even had she wished it.

Which of course she did not, and so she forced away any lingering, unwanted warmth his return had kindled within her. "How can I help you, Captain? My father won't be home for a fortnight at least. I fear it's too long for Thomas to wait."

Icy dread settled in her stomach. In truth, she *knew* his brother would not survive the length of time it would require her father to journey back to Philadelphia. If Thomas even survived the night, or another scant handful of days, it would be a miracle.

"I cannot afford to remain moored in one place for a fortnight." His regard turned sharp, deliberating. "What of *you*, Mrs. Winstead? If I recall correctly, you were ever at your father's elbow, the son he never had. Hell, I never met a woman as well-read as you, and that was years gone now. I imagine you've read dozens more books since."

"Perhaps hundreds," she confirmed before thinking better of the admission. It was rare, she knew, for a woman to be treated to the education her father had given her. She could only hope she'd proven worthy.

"Can you tend to him?" He crossed the distance between them, vibrating with intensity. "*Would* you tend to him?"

Her? Aboard a pirate ship? Amidst a band of cutthroats and scoundrels? She pressed a hand to her heart, staring at the man who had walked from her life with such calm only to return with the force of a tempest. "Good heavens, I am not a physician, Captain Grey. Can you not find someone else? My father is not the sole doctor in this city."

Edmond shook his head, his hands, large and dark with sun and roughened from life aboard a ship, seized on her arms. He was so near she could smell his scent, a decadent blend of rain and the sea and the man she had once loved. "He is the only man I would have trusted. It's far too dangerous."

"Surely you have the coin to persuade another," she persisted, attempting to withdraw from his grasp. But he was stronger, and he held firm, and she had to admit that being within his hold did not feel alarming or even wrong.

It felt…*right*. His heat and potency seeped into her through the thin fabric barrier keeping her bare skin from his. A disquieting frisson of awareness danced through her before she could tamp it down.

He lowered his head, his dark gaze searching hers for a moment, almost as if he attempted to judge whether or not he should proceed, before his brow snapped into a frown. "There is a price of one thousand pounds on my head, Mrs. Winstead. Dead or alive and preferably dead. While I could pay a considerable amount to any doctor, it would be far more worth his while to shoot me and be done with."

She gasped. The sum was an outright fortune. Why, the governor of New York only earned a wage of twelve hundred pounds per annum. "One thousand pounds?"

His jaw hardened. "Turn me in to authorities at your peril, madam."

How could he imagine she could ever turn against him? "You never knew me at all if you think me capable of such betrayal."

"Damn it." His grip tightened on her as he seemed to wage an inner battle. "Of course I trust you, Lizzie."

The way he said her name then—tinged with reverence and the remembered intimacy of their youth—softened her. Weakened her. How impossible it was to believe he was capable of committing such crimes on the sea. To imagine he had changed so much from the sweet, handsome lad who had stolen kisses from her.

In that moment, she realized he could never truly be

Captain Grey to her. He would always be *Edmond*. "Tell me what happened."

This time, he did not vacillate. "We were on our way to Maine to careen the ship. We were close to Philadelphia when the frigate attacked us. I had heard your father had come to the Colonies some time ago and settled here. I knew he was my last resort. But now it would seem that you are."

She could not deny the surge of longing within her at his words. She wanted to help him. Wished she could promise him she could heal his brother's wound. But the obstacles between them and such an outcome were insurmountable.

Lizzie shook her head. "I have never performed surgery. If the musket ball is yet in his skull, I cannot help him."

"It was a grazing blow, but infection set in."

"Infection." The dread swirling through her gathered the weight of a hundred stones, settling on her chest. Infection was tantamount to a death sentence ordinarily, let alone on a ship with no surgeon floating at sea. *Dear God.*

"Lizzie, I need your help." He released her arms and took her hands in his, a gesture that both moved and surprised her coming from a man who appeared so outwardly hardened by the life he'd chosen.

Helping a pirate was treason, whether or not he was the lost love of her youth. She could not make the decision frivolously. Indeed, she ought not to even be contemplating such a ludicrous, dangerous, foolhardy act. And yet, how could she deny a wounded man the chance to live? And how could she turn Edmond away?

Still, her mind warred with her heart. "I cannot board your ship, Captain. You are thieves at best, murderers at worst."

"I cannot move him lest it worsen his condition. You must come to the ship with me. I swear to you that you will be safe in my protection, and as soon as Thomas no longer needs your care, you will be returned to shore." His fingers tightened over hers. "Would you have me beg?"

"I find it difficult to imagine the great Captain Grey begging for anything," she said softly, still hesitant to acquiesce.

He did not flinch, keeping their fingers linked, and everywhere his skin touched hers, she burned. "For my brother's life, I would do anything."

Could she do this? Did she dare trust him? Was the potential to save one life worth risking her own? Her mind flitted over the possibilities, weighing her decision. "I know not what to say."

"Say yes," he urged, his eyes fierce and unrelenting.

She could not look away or deny him. For the first time in her life, Lizzie Winstead did something reckless. "I will help you," she blurted.

"Thank you." He released her hands and relief washed over his chiseled features, unfettered, along with another emotion that she couldn't quite define. "Thank you, Lizzie."

And then in the next instant, he cupped her face, his lips settling over hers, warm and smooth and familiar, and it was what she had wanted, what she had longed for without realizing it, only sweeter, less punishing and possessing. But just when she reached for him, it was over before it had truly begun. She found herself blinking up at him as if she had just been roused from a deep sleep. He looked down at her with an equal amount of befuddlement.

They still stood in uncomfortable proximity, and Lizzie was all too aware of the lateness of the hour, the fact that they were alone, and the limited amount of garments she wore. The burning that had begun in her palms swept through her body, settling in her core with a deep, steady thrum of longing.

She ignored it, taking a step away from him and concentrating instead on the only thing that mattered. Her patient. "Your brother remains aboard the ship now?"

"It was too risky to leave it in port given our notoriety. I ordered the crew back out to sea with plans to return for me at dawn." He raised a brow. "I thought I may have the devil of a time convincing your father to sail aboard a pirate ship with me."

"You want me to *sail* with you?" She had foolishly assumed she would tend to Thomas while the boat was anchored.

"It's necessary, I'm afraid. I can't move Thomas without doing him further harm or without making my presence here known. You'll sail with us to Maine and I'll return you on our trip south."

She was to sail on a pirate ship. Lizzie had never gone on a voyage other than her journey from England to the Colonies. She knew nothing of what to expect. The prospect seemed dangerous and imprudent for a gentlewoman accustomed to a life of ease and elegance at her father's comfortable house. But it also seemed oddly appealing.

She did not wish to consider the reason for that. No, she would not.

Lizzie cleared her throat. "I should prepare for the journey, then." Aside from medical supplies, she would need to pack some dresses, perhaps a book. "Would you like to rest? Dawn is many hours away."

He sighed, the fight seemingly drained from him. "I'd appreciate a warm bed."

"I shall have Judith get you settled then, and I'll make certain I have everything I need."

Chapter Two

*H*E HADN'T MEANT to kiss her. In the quiet of the chamber he'd been escorted to, Edmond looked out the window into the black night. Only the sound of rain pounding the slate roof could be heard. It had been a long time since he'd enjoyed the privacy of a real home. He'd sailed the world, touching land when he needed to hide, sell his spoils, or restore his supplies. In the process, he'd made a number of friends in the Colonies, and more than a few enemies who couldn't be bought.

Edmond slammed his fist into the casement, berating himself for what he'd done. She was not his, he had to remind his baser self. He had no right to want her. He had no right to be in her home with an ache in his breeches. Damn his blood, he shouldn't have touched her.

But it was there, pulsing and demanding, the pull he'd always felt for her compounded by years and a man's unslaked hunger. He'd had his share of women and none had ever compared. He'd never forgotten Lizzie Crawley. Of course, he supposed he shouldn't think of her as the innocent girl he'd abandoned any longer. What had the servant called her?

Mrs. Winstead.

His Lizzie had become another man's wife. Edmond had no justification for experiencing the acute stab of jealousy aching in his gut, but he felt it just the same. He'd given her freedom, left her to make her own happiness as he'd tried to forge his. But piracy hadn't made him happy, only wealthy. And it had proven a fickle mistress, ready to take away as swiftly as she gave.

If Thomas died, he'd never forgive himself. Although he'd long ago cast the die for a life of sin, he'd been praying ever since catching sight of Thomas bleeding on the deck. Fortunately, word traveled well amongst the settlers and he'd known for some time that Dr. Crawley had come to Philadelphia. It had been a desperate last chance.

When he'd decided to seek out Lizzie's father, he hadn't thought to find her there. He had expected she still lived an ocean away in London. Instead, his intrepid girl had followed her father to the new world. Perhaps she wasn't so different from him, he thought wryly. Perhaps she too had been struck by the hunger for travel and adventure.

But it wouldn't do to linger on thoughts of her. She was not his, never had been. He'd given up any claim on her the day he'd told her goodbye. *Damn it*, the urge to run was strong. She was the last woman in the world in whose company he could be trusted. He wanted her with a ferocity that shook him.

What a true bastard he was, he thought grimly. His brother was near death and here he stood, thinking with his cock. Disgusted, he shucked off his shirt and began pacing the room, willing his thoughts to more important matters. He could not afford to put either Lizzie or Thomas in jeopardy with his actions. And though he knew it well, he still wanted her more than he'd ever wanted any other woman, damn his hide to hell.

LIZZIE HESITATED OUTSIDE the closed chamber door. She reminded herself she was being a good hostess, making certain Edmond had been well taken care of by Judith. She'd told Judith and Jeremiah that a family member had taken ill and she was needed, that she had to travel and would return soon. To her father, she confided the truth in a letter she sealed and placed in his office. She had also gathered the medical instruments and tinctures she'd need to attend Thomas, along with a few serviceable mantuas and petticoats. It was time for sleep, but she didn't think she could.

Before she lost her courage, she knocked on his door. "Edmond? It's Lizzie."

It was unspeakably familiar of her to be calling him by his first name and knocking on his chamber door. *But this is Edmond,* her heart reminded her. Between her decision to accompany him and this moment, her barriers had seemingly diminished, leaving her vulnerable, transfixed by a delicious longing for the forbidden.

No. She must not allow herself to weaken. She was acting out of the need to help save a life alone, and not because of the feelings that had never faded for a man she did not dare trust. Lizzie was about to spin on her heel and flee to the safety of her chamber when that low, rough voice rumbled through the night and landed somewhere in the vicinity of her heart.

"Enter."

One word, that was all he said, and yet it affected her. *He* affected her. And how could he not when she opened the door to discover him naked from the waist up, his masculine body perfectly delineated in the candlelight? His chest was broad and defined, dusted with dark hair that trailed down his muscled stomach and disappeared below his breeches. His hat was gone, revealing a head of dark hair held in a queue at his nape. Strong thighs were evident beneath the tight breeches, along with the tempting outline of a part of his anatomy she ought not to notice.

Her mouth went dry and she forced her gaze to roam back up to the safety of his face before she found her voice. "D-do you require anything else before I retire?"

His gaze glittered into hers, and an unwanted, answering pang of need skated through her. "Come inside and close the door," he ordered in such a commanding tone that she obeyed.

Unnerved by his state of undress and his request both, she lingered at the door. "Do you find the chamber to your liking?"

"Of course." He took a step in her direction.

Her breath hitched. Why had she sought him out? Why did she stand here now, tempting the devil himself? *Go,* her mind screamed. *Flee before it is too late.*

But she was trapped in the twin spells of his dark eyes and powerful body. "Is there something you require?" she asked again, trying not to allow her eyes to settle on his full mouth as if she wanted another kiss. *Hopeless.* She could not help but look and admire.

"There is indeed, Lizzie." In another bare-footed step, he was close enough to touch. He slid an arm around her waist and pulled her into his hard frame. "You."

A strong pulse of desire radiated through her before she could quell it. Was this the pirate in him, thinking he could simply claim what he wanted and enjoy her as he wished? Her hands flitted to his shoulders, finding them rigid and broad, his skin hot and silken beneath her bare fingers. Though she did not push him away, she stiffened in his arms.

She would not fall prey to him. *He is a criminal,* she reminded herself. *The boy you once knew is gone.* And the man in his place was far too dangerous, far too alluring, far too everything that was sinful and wrong.

Lizzie tipped her head back in defiance. "I'm not a prize ship to be conquered."

A slow smile curved his lips, drawing her gaze to his mouth, making her think of the fleeting kiss he had given her earlier. "You're far too beautiful to be a ship, Lizzie."

"Flattery will not win me." She could not disguise her breathlessness, and it vexed her. It irked her even more that he seemed so composed, that he could reappear in the midst of a spring rainstorm as if he had never been gone from her life, and imagine she was his for the taking. Worst of all, that her traitorous body and heart *wanted* to be his.

He leaned into her, his warm breath skimming over her mouth in a parody of a kiss, and yet he made no other move. "What will?"

"Nothing." She wrenched herself from his grasp, hating herself for the weakness she had for him. For loving the boy she'd once known and wanting to forgive the man she didn't know his sins. For being tempted to remain where she was and allow him to do whatever he wished to her. She straightened her shoulders and took a breath, her gaze never faltering from his. "If there is nothing else you require, I shall bid you good evening."

Before he could respond or attempt to touch her again, she turned and fled from the room. She could not afford to become entangled with Captain Edmond Grey any more than she already was. Lizzie slipped into the hall, the soft sound of his laughter mocking her as she went.

Chapter Three

BY THE TIME the sun began its morning ascent, Lizzie found herself sailing away from Philadelphia and her quiet life of widowhood. Edmond didn't introduce her to the sun-bronzed men, a hard scrabble, unkempt lot of Frenchmen and Englishmen. Instead he took her directly to the small cabin where his brother lay at the mercy of his wounds.

The lower ship smelled of moisture and brine. It was surprisingly spacious below decks and not so different from the passenger ship she'd sailed upon from England, other than its smaller size. Unless she mistook her guess, the ship had once belonged to a wealthy merchant, until the merchant had the misfortune to run across the Scourge of the Atlantic, of course.

A rather dangerous-looking sailor watched over Thomas. He stood as she and Edmond entered, whipping a cap from his head. Under ordinary circumstances, Lizzie would have easily mistaken him for a criminal. Then again, she reminded herself that pirates were indeed criminals, merely criminals of the seas rather than the road.

Edmond wore a grim expression as he gestured to Lizzie. "Jean, this is Mrs. Winstead. She's kindly agreed to tend to Thomas for us. Mrs. Winstead, this is Jean, my first mate."

"Beg pardon, Captain," Jean began with an obvious French accent, "but a woman?"

His response did not surprise her. Most men were dubious of a learned woman. "I've trained with my father, who is a well-known physician throughout England and the Colonies. I understand your hesitation, but I can promise you I shall do my utmost to care for Thomas."

"Mrs. Winstead is to be treated to a level of respect higher than even myself," Edmond ordered. "Please convey this to the rest of the men."

She fancied it was almost unheard of for a genteel lady to be present on a pirate ship. Perhaps just as unheard of as a woman who would dare to seek an education for herself. Lizzie wanted to make it clear she was no fainting miss. She could hold her ground against this lot of toughened men.

"I'll earn their respect with my actions," she said with a confidence she didn't completely feel. After all, she knew too well no matter how much knowledge one possessed, miracles happened rarely. And her patient was in a bad way.

Her mind turned to the task before her. She crossed the cabin and knelt at Thomas' bedside, heedless of the damage it did to her skirts. The poor lighting rendered it difficult to perform a proper examination.

She glanced up. "Captain, bring the lamp closer, please?"

He did as she asked, joining her wordlessly by Thomas' sickbed. The light revealed what she had feared. Thomas' complexion was pale, his skin damp with sweat. A large, oozing wound marred his right temple. She pressed a hand to his forehead.

"He's with fever. How long has he been this way?" she asked Jean.

"Since *hier soir* he has the sweats, then the shivers."

"Last night," she murmured to herself. "That isn't good. Fevers weaken the body and he needs his strength to recover. I'll need to stave off the fever."

"Will you bleed him?" Edmond knelt at her side, his voice pained.

"Contrary to many other physicians, my father does not believe in the efficacy of bleeding a patient. No," she decided, "we will treat the fever differently. I've brought some dried marigold. Jean, if you could boil some water, I'll make a tea for Thomas to drink. I've found it helpful in reducing fever."

"Marigold tea?" Edmond sounded dubious.

She'd suspected he might have difficulty trusting in her. Lizzie placed a hand on his arm. "I study herbs. Either you trust me or you do not, but you must decide now. If you question me, it will only hinder my ability to give him proper care."

He raised a brow, his expression turning startled. "Damn feisty wench aren't you?"

"I've had to be," she said simply. "Do you trust me or not, Edmond?"

A grim frown turned down his lips. "I have little choice in the matter."

"I will do my utmost to help him." The need to reassure and comfort him rose within her, unstoppable. While he may have become a toughened pirate capable of anything, seeing his stark concern and care for his brother could not help but to pierce the armor she'd donned over her heart. She could sense his vulnerability the way she felt the sea rolling beneath them, and it moved her. Perhaps she was wrong to insist upon believing no trace of the young man she'd loved remained within his battle-hardened façade.

"It's all I ask." He swallowed and bowed his head.

"I'll need to organize myself or I won't be much good to anyone." She rose and placed her satchel on a table that had been secured to the floor. She'd brought a selection of her medicinal herbs that were dear since she'd yet to establish a reliable herb garden in her new home. She'd brought a salve of houseleek leaves to stop bleeding and wormwood conserve for herself in case she suffered from seasickness. Working with her father had taught her she'd need to cleanse the wound and keep it in clean bandages.

She plucked the flask of whiskey she'd packed from her satchel, along with some squares of muslin and the houseleek salve. "The wound has to be cleaned."

Edmond's jaw tightened, his expression severe. "Whatever must be done shall be done."

Lizzie went back to the bed, her mind galloping ahead of her. "How long has he been insensate?"

"Since taking the ball to his temple, I believe."

It was ominous news. Injuries to the head were incredibly perilous. In her experience, it was difficult for anyone to recover from a serious blow. "You must know he may never wake," she warned quietly, hating to have to deliver the sobering news.

Edmond swallowed, keeping his gaze trained on his fallen brother's still form. "I understand."

His distress was plain. She wanted to comfort him or offer encouraging words but yet she would not raise false hopes. Moreover, she could not allow herself to falter or feel. Her every action was now a matter of life and death.

Lizzie carefully tipped the flask over the wound and sent a stream of whiskey upon it. She focused on running the cloth gingerly over the injury. A fresh coating of blood oozed to the surface. She worked until she felt the wound had been thoroughly cleaned. Throughout the process, Thomas remained alarmingly still. She applied some houseleek salve to his wound, then pressed a square of cloth to his head, securing it by winding strips carefully round his forehead. By the time she finished, Jean had returned with a steaming pot of water and a cup.

"Place it on the table if you please." She rose and turned to fix the marigold tea.

Edmond stood as well. "Jean, you'll help Mrs. Winstead until she no longer requires you. Fetch me if I'm needed."

His sudden defection troubled her. She looked to him in askance. "Captain? I thought you would aid me."

"Jean is more than capable." His tone had turned dismissive. Curt. "I've a ship to captain, Mrs. Winstead."

She told herself it did not matter, that any tentative bond she'd felt burgeoning between herself and the Scourge of the Atlantic should never be allowed to flourish anyway. Like a weed in her herb garden, it must be plucked. Besides, she had far graver concerns than the whims of a notorious pirate.

She had a patient who needed her, and that was all that mattered.

EDMOND STALKED THE deck of the *Freedom*, cursing himself. He hadn't meant to treat Lizzie with such coldness. But damn his eyes, watching helplessly as his brother slipped closer to death with each breath was more than he could bear. He did have a ship to captain, and above decks he could feel the ocean breeze, watch the rugged beauty of the sea around him. He was at home. Allowing himself to entertain tenderness toward Lizzie was foolhardy. He could never be happy anywhere but aboard his ship.

Ollie, his gunner, approached him, wearing a look of concern. "Captain, we're being followed."

Damn. He couldn't afford another battle, not now with Lizzie aboard and Thomas so close to death. "Sodding hell, this is not what we need. How far off and can you tell who the devil it is?"

"Looks as if it's English colors, just over there." Ollie gestured to a speck on the horizon that was unmistakably the silhouette of another ship.

His own countrymen wanted him dead. It was a sobering thought. With the price on his head, navigating the waters he'd come to know like the palm of his hand became more treacherous by the day. Every man with a frigate at his disposal was trying to hunt down the *Freedom*. They'd earned their enemies the hard way, taking more ships than Edmond had even bothered to count.

"Another bastard wanting a piece of us, do you think?" He stroked his beard, already strategizing. He excelled at battle, and in its fiery depths, he could lose himself, forget about the sight of his brother so damn pale and still below.

"Very likely, Captain." Ollie grinned, showing a row of teeth as brown as the planks beneath his feet. "We'll take them on, no problem. Always do."

They were fighters, the men of the *Freedom*. They'd all seen their fair share of hell. Many of them had been pressed into the navy against their will. Others had been assured pay by unscrupulous merchants who never fulfilled their promises. Still others had joined their ranks from the ships they'd plundered.

Together they had become a menace so great that the cry for them to be stopped had been raised as far away as London. The Governor of Virginia wanted Edmond's head on a pike. None of them were yet ready to stop pirating. It was in their blood. It was the only life they'd come to know.

His mind churned. "How many grenades have we?"

"I had the lads working up more through the night," Ollie replied. "We emptied a few rum bottles to aid in the task. It was a hardship, but we managed."

Edmond laughed. They'd long ago discovered a grand use for the rum bottles they drained. Stuffed with gunpowder and bits of metal, they made formidable weapons. "A hardship indeed. If you're ready, we'll bide our time and let them come to us."

Ollie nodded. "Yes, sir."

But as the day wore on, the approaching ship slipped from their sight. Perhaps they weren't to be attacked by an enemy ship after all, the men reckoned. Edmond wasn't convinced. He watched and waited, an uneasy sensation settling in his bones. He had a feeling they hadn't seen the last of the ship on the horizon.

Chapter Four

$\mathcal{L}$IZZIE ENDURED A long, wearying day of tending to Thomas. As the hours dragged by, she expected Edmond to return and inquire after his brother's welfare, but he disappointed her. Jean was a man of few words but nevertheless proved himself an invaluable help. Together they spooned marigold tea and fresh broth between their patient's lips. She cleansed his wound repeatedly. By nightfall, Thomas' fever appeared to have broken for good. She deemed it an excellent time to allow herself an hour or two of rest.

Jean guided her to a cabin where, as she discovered the moment the door closed behind him, she was about to face yet another battle. Edmond was within, seated, a bottle of rum at his side. He didn't bother to acknowledge her presence but she knew he was as aware of her as she was of him. Before the door even closed at Jean's back, the tension emanating between them hung heavier than the scent of seawater in the air.

Edmond took a swig directly from the bottle, staring into the planked floors. "How is he?"

"Thomas is improving." She stayed close to the door, uncertain of his mood. He appeared raffish at the moment. "He has yet to wake, but his fevers have subsided."

"Will he live?"

"I don't know," she answered honestly.

"You needn't linger at the door as if I'm about to accost you." His voice, like his countenance, was forbidding.

"I don't fear you, Edmond." She took a step closer to prove her point, realizing as she said the words how true they were. Try as she might to view him as a murderous criminal, she had witnessed his vulnerability. He had put his life in jeopardy in an attempt to save his brother's. There was good to him, undeniable good, and she could no longer convince herself that he was a scoundrel unworthy of her care. "To others you may be a pirate, but to me you are merely a man."

He swigged another gulp of rum, his dark, glittering stare burning into hers. "You'll need some rest, I expect. I will sleep on the floor if you wish it."

She moved closer again, taking in his appearance, haggard and ashen in his worry. Seeing his brother's condition had affected him. Thomas was in a bad way, she knew. But she also believed in the efficacy of knowledge, of medicine well researched and practiced. Her father had spent scores of his life perfecting his science. She possessed only a scant handful of his education, but she believed in his methods. She believed saving Thomas' life was possible, especially since the fevers had gone.

"Thomas will have a fighting chance," she promised Edmond, understanding him perhaps better than she ever had in that moment. "You've done your duty in seeing to that."

"How have I done my duty?" He roared the words, shooting to his feet to stalk across the length of the cabin. "Answer me that, Lizzie. Damn my blood, how have I done my duty when my younger brother lies on his deathbed at this moment?"

Something shifted inside her then. Her heart ached for him. His pain was palpable, obvious. Others would likely find it difficult to believe the feared Scourge of the Atlantic possessed a heart. Had she not known him in their youths, Lizzie would have had the same belief. But she knew him, knew his vulnerability was real and not affected. Thomas meant a great deal to Edmond, and he felt responsible for Thomas' grave condition.

She went to him, almost afraid of the anger emanating from his strong body but knowing she had to attempt to give him solace. She closed the distance between them, placed her hands on his stiff shoulders. "Edmond, you cannot carry on this way. It does no service to either yourself or your brother."

"To hell with your soft woman's words," he scoffed, shrugging from her touch.

She gathered her courage and matched his angry strides even in the constraints of her mantua and petticoats. "To hell with nothing, Edmond Grey. Listen to me. Did you force your brother to join you?"

"Christ, no. He followed me without my knowledge or consent, thinking a pirate's life a rum adventure. The truth is this life isn't for anyone who wants to live beyond the next plunder. One mistake and everything we've earned, all the prizes and glorious ships we've overtaken, each battle we've won, is gone. In the end, pirate or no, you're just a goddamn head on a pike." His voice broke. "I warned him. I bloody well warned him."

His back was to her. Without speaking, she followed him. Tentatively, she wound her arms around his waist, holding him, knowing instinctively it was what he needed. Perhaps what she needed as well.

The night was silent around them but for the gusting of wind and slosh of waves. The ship pitched but she was fortunate to not yet suffer the ill effects of seasickness. She'd seemed to have found her balance. It hadn't been that long since she'd made the long passage from England to the

Americas.

"Why must you persist in being so damn kind and good?" He turned suddenly in her arms and yanked her against him. His reaction was almost violent in his passion. His eyes shone like twin pieces of coal. "Why, Lizzie?"

Before she could answer, his mouth was on hers. The kiss was fierce, insistent. It claimed, it took. He slanted his firm lips over hers, his tongue sliding into the wet recesses of her mouth, plundering the same way he would a ship. She opened to him, giving willingly, because she could no longer deny what remained between them, undiminished by years and distance.

Her tongue mated with his. Her every sense was on edge, aware of his masculine scent, the way he tasted like spice, his hands caressing her bottom through the layers of her dress. She was wet, throbbing between her legs, hungry for him to claim her. Needing him to. The emotions she'd managed to hold at bay, the restlessness, the pent-up longing, unleashed. She was helpless. Unable to stop, to fight, to resist.

To think of all the reasons why wanting the Scourge of the Atlantic was wrong.

She cupped his face, relishing the sensation of his rough beard on her fingertips. She wanted him with a savagery that frightened her. The magnetism between them was powerful yet new to her. While she'd been wed to Richard for three years, their life together had been complacent, comfortable. He had been content to wade through his books, she to care for their home. Although they'd shared a quiet affection, there had been no passion.

This was different in every way. It was wild. Thrilling.

Edmond pulled the sash from her mantua and pushed the heavy brocade from her body. The pins holding her stomacher in place tinkled as they hit the floor. He slid his hands from her waist to her breasts, weighing each one in his hands. Her nipples puckered and poked against the thin fabric of her smock.

He broke the kiss, meeting her gaze. "I swore to myself I wouldn't touch you. Tell me to stop."

"I don't want you to stop," she confessed.

"I have nothing to offer you. I'm a wanted man, Lizzie."

He was a pirate, a man who took risks with his life each day. She was not naïve in giving her body to him. Perhaps it was wrong, but for the first time, she felt needed. It was a rare, extraordinary thing.

"I haven't asked you for anything more than what you're free to give."

With a groan, he began working on her petticoat. She helped him off with his shirt. They were suddenly half nude, frantic. Kissing and stripping away each other's garments, they made their way to his narrow bed. They fell upon it naked. Lizzie tore her mouth from his and pushed him to his back. Though he was far stronger than she, he allowed her control over him and the realization heightened her pleasure. She dropped a series of kisses down his neck, over his muscled chest, moving lower still. His cock was stiff and ready.

She wanted to take him in her mouth and give him pleasure, to grant him release from the weary heaviness of his worries. When her hand wrapped around his thick shaft, he moaned and jerked his hips. An answering blossom of heat unfurled in her. She took the tip of him in her mouth, running her tongue over his satiny skin in circular whorls. Then she sucked, taking as much of him as she could. Guided by instinct, she mimicked the motions of lovemaking, stroking him with her mouth as she sucked and licked. His breathing became ragged as he struggled to maintain control.

"Lizzie, sweet Christ. I won't last much longer."

She didn't care. She wanted to bring him to release with her mouth, to taste him. Sucking his cock left her wet and aching between her legs. It was delicious and debauched. She loved the heaviness of him on her tongue, the moans she wrung from him.

"Come here to me," he growled.

Lizzie glanced up the solid length of his body and met his gaze. "Tell me what you want me to do," she whispered.

"Come and I'll show you." Wicked intent underscored his tone, glimmered in his dark eyes.

She rose to her knees and scooted away from his tempting cock. He gripped her waist with one hand and her thigh with another. "Turn around and sit astride me." He helped her to position herself, arranging her so that she was on her knees, one leg bent on either side of his chest. "Now rise. I want to taste you while you suck my cock."

Lizzie did as he instructed. His tongue dipped inside her, making her cry out. Nothing could have prepared her for the sweet, sinful seduction of Edmond's mouth upon her intimate flesh. She lowered her head to take his beautiful cock in her mouth again. His tongue teased the bud of her sex, plumping the aching nub. He sucked it between his teeth. She laved his cock with her tongue, panting, mindless with pleasure. He rubbed his face in her folds, his beard abrading her delicate skin. His cock was slippery with her saliva, her sex soaked by his ministrations.

Just as she feared she'd lose herself, he groaned and tore his mouth from her. "Enough. If I don't have you soon, I'll go mad."

Lizzie rose, allowing him to guide her until she faced him. In the low light, she could see the slick sheen of her juices on his sensual lips. He reached between them, probing her entrance with his stiff cock. "Take me inside you."

She ground her hips against his in response. He thrust upward, his cock impaling her in one swift motion. His big hands anchored her waist, helping her to begin a rhythm. She rode his shaft, taking him inside, then lifting so that he almost slipped from her body before pulling him back in once more. His eyes closed, his expression one of relaxed gratification.

"That's right, my girl. Ride me as hard as you like. I'm all yours."

At his words, she began a faster pace, loving the feel of him within her, loving the sense of control being the dominant partner gave her. She wanted more, faster. She never wanted to stop. He rocked his hips beneath her, deepening the penetration. His right hand slid from her hip, coming between them to play with her sex. She tightened on him instantly, pleasure shooting through her body.

"Fuck me, sweet Lizzie," he growled, rocking into her.

With a throaty moan she continued sliding over his cock, each jerk of her hips bringing them both closer to release. The wet sounds of their lovemaking filled the chamber. Lizzie reached her pinnacle again, gripping him so tightly with her passage that he came too, pumping his seed inside her. He swiveled his hips, getting as deep as he could, filling her. Gasping for breath, her body covered in a sheen of perspiration, she collapsed at his side.

His arm slid around her, drawing her to him. "I cannot give you enough thanks for all you've done for Thomas this day."

Was their lovemaking nothing more than his appreciation for her efforts on his brother's behalf? Not liking the thought, she drew her head up to gaze at him. He was beautiful in a rakish sense, his hair a wild black tangle around him. His eyes sparked into hers.

"I do not require your gratitude," she informed him. "If

that is all you feel—"

He pressed a finger to her lips. "Don't say another word or you'll make a fool of us both."

He was right, she knew. Why complicate what they shared? They were two people with an appreciation for each other, two people both a bit lost in their own worlds. Why not seek comfort in each other? Why not taste passion before returning to her life of loneliness?

"Forgive me," she murmured, dropping a kiss on his chest.

He ran his hand over her hair in a comforting caress. "Always, Lizzie. You've been an angel since the day I met you."

"Surely not such an angel or you wouldn't have gone off to sea." She tried to keep the edge from her voice but could not.

"If I had stayed and married you, neither of us would have been happy. Even I knew that much, stupid lad that I was. I have roaming in my soul. I was made to sail these seas until they claim me. It would've been pure selfishness to subject you to my way of life."

"Would you never like to call one place your home?" She knew she shouldn't ask, that it was certainly not her place to pry. But she couldn't resist. Part of her had wondered ever since he'd left.

"The sea is my home and mistress both," he said simply.

She was left with the same dismaying realization that had struck her all those years ago. Although she'd loved him with uncompromising fervor, Edmond Grey was not capable of loving anyone but the sea. Trying to ignore the pang in her heart, she shifted away from him. If she wanted to keep her feelings from being dashed once again, she'd do well to keep her distance.

"I should like to check on Thomas again." She rose and began scooping up her discarded garments. Best to stay the course she knew and stay far from the one she didn't else she'd be facing the same sad ending she'd experienced ten years before. And she'd be standing alone as she watched Edmond Grey walk out of her life.

Chapter Five

$\mathcal{E}$DMOND WATCHED LIZZIE pick up her garments. Her body was truly a thing of beauty. She'd matured and bloomed into the breathtaking woman he'd always known she would be. He'd never thought to see her again, and now he'd lain with her. He should not have allowed his baser urges to overcome his judgment. She was having difficulty keeping her emotions at bay and he could sense it.

"Lizzie, I've been honest with you."

"Of course you have." There were tears in her voice as she threw on a shift, ending his view of her tempting backside. "You've always been the same Edmond Grey, and I've always been helpless to resist you."

"If I could be the man you need, I would." Christ, he could still smell her on his skin, in his bed. He felt just as helpless as she claimed to be.

"Think nothing of it," she said quietly, pulling on her dress. "I have a patient to attend." With that, she was gone.

He had to go to her. He knew it the moment she left the cabin. Damn it, he was making a mess of things, allowing their intimacy to go so far, allowing her to once again have hopes for a future with him. He couldn't hurt her a second time.

He stood and slapped on a pair of breeches and a shirt, cursing himself for the worst sort of scoundrel. He had no right to bring unhappiness to her. He didn't want to be the cause of the sadness in her pretty eyes. She deserved far better than a worthless bastard like him. But he was damned if he knew how to make peace between them.

SHE'D NEARLY MADE it to Thomas' sick room when a pair of hands clamped on her waist. With a muffled shriek, she spun about, prepared to do battle. She didn't trust the pirates one bit, despite any threats Edmond may have made to them regarding her safety. Her heart kicked a beat when she realized Edmond had followed her.

He hauled her against his chest. "Why do you run from me, Lizzie?"

It was true. She had been running. Her emotions for him were too raw, too real, a jumbled hodgepodge of old clashing with new. "I have a patient to care for if you'll recall," she reminded him.

"I'm aware of that." He tipped up her chin. "But Jean is keeping watch over him with orders to fetch us if Thomas' condition changes. You've done what you could. Working yourself to weakness won't help him."

"I can take care of myself," she told him. The need for some distance between them was a strong urge.

"While you're on my ship, I'm responsible for your welfare."

Her patience snapped like a weak thread. "If that's indeed true, you're failing miserably. I'm the most in danger when in your presence."

He released her. "If you don't want to suffer my attentions, you need only say the words."

Her heart ached, mind warring with common sense and

confusion and, worst of all, the love that had always been simmering beneath the surface of her heart. All for him, only for him. "I don't understand you, Edmond."

"Christ, I don't understand myself."

He reached for her hand, but she pulled it from his grasp. "Don't."

"Ah." A pained smile curved his lips. "Have you regained your senses then?"

It hurt her to deny him, truly it did, but her own self-preservation had to win the day. She was not, could never be, as world weary as he. "I think it unwise for us to proceed in such a foolhardy manner. I lost my head."

"Well, best you lose yours before I lose mine."

Lizzie lost her temper. "Stop it at once."

He raised a brow, impassive as ever. "Stop what?"

"Jesting about your demise as if it were an amusing parlor sally. Haven't you heard about all the pirates who've been killed? Bad enough your own brother lies dying. It seems you're bent on killing yourself as well." Anger mingled with frustration. She slapped at his coat, wanting to make him see reason. "Bless your poor mother. She must be a saint for all this."

"My mother is dead," he bit out. "I don't think she gives a damn."

She felt the lash of his words like a blow. He had worshipped his mother, and she understood that her loss would have devastated him.

Even so, the knowledge of his mother's passing didn't render Lizzie any less frustrated. "She may not, but I do care," she lashed at him. "I *care*, Edmond. What happened to make you into the man you've become? What made you so cold?"

"Seeing hell." His tone was grim. "Living through one battle after the next. Almost dying. You've lived your pretty life without a bit of discomfort or misfortune."

"How dare you?" Rage coursed through her. "Do you think I was fortunate to nurse my husband through illness? To watch helplessly each day as he faded away? Do you think it was *comfortable* to be left with nothing, to have to depend upon my father for my bread once more?"

His stare was intense, blazing. Silence reigned in the wake of her outburst for several beats before he broke it.

"It is my turn to beg your pardon. Forgive me, Lizzie." Sincerity laced his voice. "I hadn't realized."

She attempted to inure herself against his sudden softening. "You may be the feared Captain Grey, but you aren't the only person on this earth who has ever been through difficult times or who has ever known pain and hurt."

"Lizzie, look at me." He caught her around the waist when she would have turned away, pulling her to him. His hand was firm on her chin, his brown gaze trapping hers. "I'm an arse."

Though she hated herself for it, her anger began dissipating. "You needn't have told me. I already knew."

He laughed then, a bitter bark that had nothing to do with levity. "How is it a slip of a woman can bring me so low?"

That she, Lizzie Winstead, would have such power over a man such as he seemed impossible. She would not have believed it so, were he not in her arms, looking down at her as if she were…as if she were somehow necessary to him.

Surely not. Surely that was wishful thinking on her part.

She shook her head, belatedly recalling his question. "I cannot answer that, Edmond. Only you can."

With a groan, he lowered his mouth to hers. Her resolve had been short-lived. But as quickly as the fires of desire ignited, they were doused as the ship gave a great heave beneath them, sending Lizzie to her knees. Edmond caught her up in his arms, holding her against him.

The hollers of men could be heard above them, mingling with the sudden roar of the sea.

"What is happening?" she asked Edmond, fear roiling through her stomach.

"A storm." Edmond's jaw was a tight line, his tone grim.

"So quickly?"

He nodded. "Get into the cabin with Thomas and don't leave unless I come for you."

"But Edmond—"

"On this I am quite firm, Lizzie. I need to keep both of you safe, and there's no telling what manner of storm this is. We've already taken a battering from the battle and we can hardly afford to withstand much more."

Another wave hit, sending the ship lolling to her side. Lizzie would have fallen if not for Edmond's grip on her. She allowed him to rush her to Thomas' cabin. The belly of the ship groaned and creaked around them, giving voice to the fright coursing through her.

Jean rose from Thomas' side at their entrance. "Captain, the storm, she is an angry one."

"God's blood, you can say that again. I'll need all hands on deck, Jean. Mrs. Winstead will stay with Thomas."

He pulled Lizzie to him and dropped a quick kiss on her mouth. "Promise me you'll stay here."

She nodded, shock and fear warring with a new barrage of emotions. "I promise."

Edmond nodded, his expression fierce, that of a man going into battle. "I'll come back to you as soon as I can. Jean?"

And then the two men were gone, leaving Lizzie to await her fate as the ship rocked helplessly in the tempest about to besiege them all.

Chapter Six

$\mathcal{E}$DMOND STOMPED INTO the storm expecting the worst and finding it. Above deck, the situation was a grave one. Men scrambled on the deck together, trying to secure the jibs and maintain the proper direction. The storm possessed an inherent, virulent fury that shook even a seasoned sailor like Edmond. He'd lived through his share of storms, but this one seemed unholy bad.

He and Jean went into action, taking up the quarterdeck and shouting commands above the din of the roaring sea. Tremendous waves rose and fell twenty feet or more in height, crashing down on the deck. It was treacherous work to remain standing and not be lost forever to the ocean. The winds had grown with astounding strength, putting the ship's sails in peril.

There was no help for it, Edmond realized. They couldn't fight the storm. All they could do was give in, which meant following the winds. They'd have to give up on Maine and head south, back into the dangerous territory of the Chesapeake. The Governor of Virginia wanted him dead. It would be foolhardy to head there so soon, but they had no other option.

Another wave slapped the *Freedom*, sending a cascade of seawater over her deck. He called out to Jean. Under ordinary conditions, he knew the *Freedom's* hull was leaky, let alone under the pressure of high seas. It wouldn't do to take on too much water.

He called out to Jean, "Get to the pumps. We're taking on water, and tell all hands we need them to man the sails. We'll have to go south with the wind or it'll tear them all to hell."

"South, sir?" Jean looked at him in askance. "That cannot be wise, no?"

"Wiser than sending us all to the bottom of the ocean," he replied with grim determination. "We'll have to take our chances with the devil we know."

Jean nodded and left the quarterdeck to Edmond, carrying out his orders. It was then, as the winds and waves kicked up a battle to beat the Armada all around him, that a crippling comprehension struck him. One thought more than the possibility of drowning, the chance his ship would break apart and sink to a watery perdition, or the thought of losing his friends overboard, slammed home. One thought more than any other shook him to his core.

He had to survive this night, if only to save the woman he loved.

Damn my blood, he silently cursed. He'd spent the last ten years scouring the ocean in search of himself, but he'd never been able to escape the one inevitable lure that brought every man to his knees.

A woman.

His woman.

The only woman he'd ever loved.

LIZZIE DIDN'T KNOW how much time passed in the grip of the storm. Thunderous waves sent her reeling to the floor more than once. She tried to keep her mind from the possibility that the ship could sink, taking her down with it, by tending to her patient. She did her utmost to keep Thomas comfortable. The oil in the lamp had burned low by the time Thomas began stirring.

His eyes opened slowly to reveal the same penetrating dark stare as his older brother's. "What?" he croaked.

Hope blossomed within her. Surely it was a good sign that he'd regained consciousness. Surely the good Lord would not cast them all to the bottom of the ocean after performing a miracle. She pressed a cup of water to his lips and helped him to take a few steadying sips.

"Hush now," she crooned. "Conserve your strength. I'm Lizzie, an old friend of your brother's. I believe we met on several occasions."

"I remember you." His halting voice was rusty with disuse and a tongue made slow by many days of illness. "It…hasn't been that many…years. How the hell…did you come to be on this ship?"

She smiled at his bold question. It too was a good sign. His thoughts seemed sharp. "You were injured in battle. Your ship's surgeon was killed, so your brother sought out my father to assist you. But my father was away, and I'm afraid you were left with me instead."

"My head feels like it's been stuck…on a goddamn pike."

"Indeed." She offered him some more water. "I assure you it hasn't."

"I suppose I owe you," he took another greedy gulp, "thanks?"

"You owe your brother thanks," she refuted. "He put his life at risk to save yours."

He closed his eyes, clearly drained from his illness. "You have my gratitude."

The ship listed again, this time with less force. She hoped the winds and waves above had calmed. Her stomach churned quite violently with the upheaval the storm had produced.

"You're welcome, Thomas."

He remained quiet for a few moments. Just when she thought he'd fallen back asleep, he shocked her with a troubling question. "Are you still in love with my brother?"

Her gaze shot to his but his eyes were yet closed. "I'm afraid I don't know what you're speaking of."

His eyes opened again. "Let's be honest, shall we, Lizzie? Unless I miss my guess, there's a storm brewing above deck that's about to pitch us to the bottom of the sea. There is no need for falsehoods."

"You're certainly garrulous for a man newly rescued from death." She didn't mean to sound so contrary, but she couldn't help it.

"You're the one who performed the rescuing," he pointed out in a good-natured tone that belied the fatigue he so obviously fought.

The ship gave another violent toss. The hull groaned as Lizzie went sprawling. She righted herself, effectively sobered. "Very well. It does seem we're in dire straits."

"You saved me so I can become food for the fishes." He gave her a halfhearted grin. "Kind of you."

"I hope not." Fear welled up within her, as powerful as the waves that could be heard crashing on the decks above. "Thomas?"

"Yes, Lizzie?"

"I have two confessions to make. The first is that I'm terribly frightened just now." She paused, weighing the wisdom of her next words. "And the second is that I never stopped loving Edmond."

"I thought as much."

A niggling worry asserted itself. "Thomas, has he anyone who loves him? A wife or a mistress somewhere?"

"Edmond has no one waiting for his return."

Relief slid through her. She had initially assumed he was unattached, but she wanted to be certain. Never would she want to pine after a man who already belonged to another woman. It would be even more reckless than pining after a pirate captain already was. Yes, she had to admit to herself she was the worst sort of fool. Perhaps in the light of day, with her life in a much more tenable position, she would regain her sanity.

Another wave assailed them, tearing a gasp from her throat. Her demise was a real possibility, and the thought was most sobering.

"Take my hand," Thomas said quietly, reaching toward her. "I haven't prayed in a long time, but I think we should now."

She linked her fingers with his and bowed her head, adding a silent prayer of her own for the captain roaming the decks of their besieged ship.

Chapter Seven

$\mathcal{A}$ SEEMINGLY LONG, though indeterminate gap of time stretched between the last vestiges of the storm and the moment Edmond stalked back through the door. Lizzie jumped up at his entrance. He was soaked through, his shirt torn open, blood streaming from a cut on his shoulder. He looked weary and battered.

"Edmond." She went to him, rushing into his arms. She didn't care if he smelled of the sea or if he dampened her own dress. Nothing mattered but that he was here with her. He'd survived. They'd all survived. It was the second miracle of the evening. His arms tightened around her and he buried his face in her hair.

"You're safe," she whispered, scarcely believing their good fortune.

"My God, Lizzie, I thought I'd never see you again." He pulled away and dropped a quick, hard kiss on her mouth. "I swear to Christ that storm came directly from the devil himself."

"Felicitations to you too, brother." Thomas' wry drawl interrupted their impromptu reunion.

Flushing, Lizzie stepped out of Edmond's embrace. Her emotions had overcome her. She'd already forgotten Thomas' presence when just minutes before, she'd been redressing his wound.

"Thomas, damn you, you're awake." A grin replaced the somber downward tilt of Edmond's lips. He crossed the room and delivered a sound clap to his brother's shoulder that left Thomas grimacing. "I thought you were going to die, you bastard."

"Easy on the brotherly concern, Eddie. I've still got the devil of a headache."

"I'm of half a mind to give you another headache," Edmond muttered. "If you ever take a musket ball for me again, I'll bloody well kill you."

Understanding dawned on Lizzie. That certainly explained Edmond's despair and anger with himself. Thomas had obviously been protecting his older brother when he'd suffered the wound. She pressed her hand over her heart, touched by watching the two men interact. Little wonder Edmond had been so devastated.

Thomas gave a halfhearted laugh. "It's my duty to look after my brother. You sure as hell don't look after yourself."

"That's my business, puppy." Edmond's tone was affectionate. It was clear the two brothers loved and respected each other very much.

"I understand thanks are in order for bringing an angel to rescue me." Thomas looked to Lizzie. "She performed a miracle on this old body of mine."

"Not so old yet." Edmond turned, his gaze on hers sending an answering flood of warmth through her. "With any luck, thanks to Mrs. Winstead, you'll be blessed enough to live to be an old man in truth." He looked back to his brother. "You just have to quit pirating."

"Go to hell," Thomas scoffed. "I'll quit when I see fit."

"Watch yourself, brother. You'll quit if I throw you off my ship," Edmond warned.

"You don't scare me, Eddie. This is *our* ship. The other

men would have to vote in favor of leaving me and I don't think they would."

Edmond heaved a sigh that sounded bone-deep. "You're right, damn your blood."

Thomas just grinned. "Now, if you don't mind, I'm in the mood for a nap and you stink like a moldy barrel of salt cod."

Lizzie couldn't help but laugh, which earned her a glare from Edmond. "'Twas your brother who said it, not I," she defended.

She was feeling suddenly dizzy with relief and fatigue both. She hadn't slept all night and it was likely soon morning. The stress of caring for Thomas and fearing that any second they'd be cast to the bottom of the sea had drained the fight from her. She was incredibly grateful for the second chance she'd been given, but all she wanted now was a warm bed and a few hours of precious slumber. The only flaw was having to share a bed with Edmond, who, moldy barrel of salt cod odor notwithstanding, was as dangerously compelling to her as ever.

"We'll leave the devil to his rest, then," Edmond murmured, his stare deepening to obsidian.

"I'll check on you in the morning," she promised Thomas. "Call for me if you should need me before then."

"Many thanks to you, Lizzie." Thomas' eyes had already closed.

She left the room with Edmond's hand possessive and firm on her waist. The hull was wet, she noticed, sea foam sprayed here and there. She raised her skirts to prevent them from being dirtied.

"How bad was the storm damage?" she asked, concern returning to her now the shock of survival had fled her.

"Several men went overboard." His jaw tightened. "We

took a beating. We'll have to stop in daylight as soon as we can to repair her."

"I'm sorry." She reached for his hand, giving his fingers a reassuring squeeze. She couldn't imagine how awful it must have been to watch his comrades being swept to sea, no way to save them.

"It could have been far worse," he said. "I've known entire ships to go down in storms like the one that just pummeled us. It's one of the hazards of the sea."

"Just the same, I'm sure it's never easy, losing men."

"Nothing worthwhile is ever easy." He gave her a sad smile.

"Isn't it? I'm not so sure." She thought of their brief time together. Giving herself to Edmond had been easy, yes. And worthwhile? Her foolish heart, thumping madly in her breast, thought so.

"Indeed." He escorted her to the privacy of his cabin. "Thomas is calling you Lizzie now, is he? You're certainly familiar with him."

Lizzie suppressed a smile of her own. "You needn't fear I've developed tender affections for your brother, Edmond. I'm yours."

The words escaped her before she could think better of them or call them back. He stiffened, looking down at her with a questioning gaze. "Are you mine, sweet Lizzie?"

"In this moment," she replied with honesty.

"And what of the next moment?" He ran a finger down her cheek.

Lizzie pressed a kiss to the pad of his finger, heart full of longing. "The choice is yours, I suppose."

He drew her to him for a kiss. She ran her palms up his chest between them, not minding if he smelled of the sea. She wanted to be as close to him as possible. She wanted him inside her. To her, in the brief span of time since his resurgence in her life, he had become as necessary as air.

Her hand landed in the unmistakable stickiness of drying blood. He was injured. How had she forgotten?

"Your wound," she cried, pulling away from his embrace. "I must tend to it at once. What happened?"

"Splintering wood." He shrugged. "I'll live."

"Let me have a look, if you please." She was already slipping the tattered remnants of his shirt down over his shoulder.

A menacing red gash stretched across his chest, still oozing blood. Her heart beat twice its rhythm. "This needs cleaning, Edmond, else I'll be nursing you as well."

Her father had taught her that wounds were always to be kept clean. Many physicians suggested strong emotion led to fevers, but her father and some of his colleagues believed otherwise.

Edmond flashed her a wicked grin. "I'm not concerned for my welfare, Lizzie darling, but you may continue removing my garments if you'd like."

"Wicked man." Trying to keep her mind on practical matters, she pushed him to the bed. "What am I to do with you?"

His grin deepened. "Get naked with me."

She tsked. "Where do you keep your rum?"

"Brilliant idea. It's in the cabinet just over there."

Lizzie fetched the half-empty bottle and tore a strip from her petticoat. It wasn't as clean as she would have preferred, but it would have to do. She splashed some rum on the muslin. "I'm afraid my idea isn't quite the same as yours."

"Why the bloody hell are you pouring my rum on a scrap of petticoat?" He sounded outraged.

She wasn't concerned. She dabbed at his wound, cleaning it as best she could despite the hiss of breath he inhaled at her touch.

"That bloody well stings, woman."

"Good." She sent him a saucy look "That means it's doing its proper job."

"Damn you, give me that bottle." He plucked the rum from her grasp before she could stop him.

"You're a most vexing patient, Captain Grey."

He hooked his free arm around her waist, drawing her into his lap. "You can call me the Scourge of the Atlantic, my love."

She laughed at his rakish charm, enjoying the easiness between them now, craving it, for however long it would last. The storm and her precarious proximity to death had changed her, had altered the way she saw Edmond. The way she allowed herself to feel for him. "You're incorrigible." She said the last without any heat.

"Absolutely," he agreed before sealing their mouths in a hungry kiss.

Lizzie kissed him back with all the repressed emotion of the past few hours. She wanted to hold him against her, to become one with him. She wanted his naked skin, his hard cock deep inside her. She wanted his tongue, his seed pumping into her. Here and now, in his arms, she felt alive. It was disconcerting and heady at the same time.

He tore his lips from hers. "I want you, Lizzie. I want you like I've never wanted another woman in my life."

"I want you too," she confessed. She wanted him so much it scared her, for the potential for ruin was as great as that of the storm they'd survived. More than anything, she wanted to believe there could be hope for them, that he wouldn't again abandon her in favor of the sea. That she could somehow surmount the impediments of life as a pirate's woman.

Was it impossible?

Could she?

Could *they*?

He smiled, framing her face with his hands. "You are so lovely. There's nothing I'd like better than taking you right here on this bed."

She didn't even think. Simply spoke. "Then perhaps you should."

"Ah, you tempt me." Edmond pressed his forehead to hers. "But I have it on good authority that I stink, and I should hate to sully you."

She inhaled, and all she could smell was *him*. Musky and earthy and necessary. "You don't truly smell. Your brother was having you on."

"Mayhap, but I'd like to clean up a bit all the same."

The urge to tend to him rose within her. She wanted to take care of him, make him feel loved. Beneath his thick pirate skin, she sensed there waited a man who wanted to know tenderness in his life once more. To know the tenderness she had long held for him in her heart but had never been able to show him. "Let me bathe you."

"You seek to spoil me," he said, but his protestation lacked bite.

"You need spoiling," she pointed out, warming to her task. "Who's been looking after you all these years?"

She couldn't help but think of him as a dory floating in the middle of the ocean, all alone, no shores in sight. Surely he longed for a home, a woman who loved him. She hadn't realized just how lonely she'd been until Edmond reappeared in her life, reawakening her to passion and possibilities.

"I've been looking after myself."

"Little wonder you're in the straits you're in." She tsked. "Pirate trying to outlast the dangers of the sea. Does it not grow old for you?"

He raised a brow. "You dare to henpeck me, my dear?"

"I am no longer the same girl you left behind." The old Lizzie had hardened into the woman she was now. "I am bolder and stronger than I was then."

Chapter Eight

$\mathcal{G}$OD'S BLOOD, SHE was right. The woman she had become was not meek and sweet but fiery in her determination, fearless enough to follow him to sea. Edmond grinned, feeling the weight settled upon his shoulders by Thomas' wounding and the storm lift merely by being in her presence. She was a saucy wench, strong enough to love without being loved in return. He'd treated her poorly in the past, and he wanted her to know, but the words escaped him.

Instead of telling her what he ought, he tilted up her chin. "If henpecked I must be, then I choose you to do the henpecking every time, my dear. I submit to your ministrations. I fetched some water earlier, just over there."

An answering smile curved her lips. "I'm relieved to hear it, Edmond." She rose and crossed the cabin, heading to the small crock of water he'd brought from the galley.

He watched the sway of her hips, thought about how sweet and hot she felt around his cock, and was instantly hard. Christ, he hoped the water was cold or he'd ravish her before she even managed to wipe the sea stench from his body. She turned back to him, cloth and crock in hand, catching the direction of his heated stare.

"How have you come to be so bloody beautiful?" he asked, content to watch her, to savor her presence.

Her eyes glinted. "How have you come to be so handsome?"

"Handsome?" He rubbed his hand over his beard. "I'm a timeworn sailor, not the sort of man you deserve."

"I'll decide that," she said simply, seating herself at his side. "You've always been my fate, Edmond Grey. You were just too stubborn to see it."

He felt her words like a knife. "I was acting in your best interest. Good Lord, Lizzie, would you have wanted to be the wife of the most wanted criminal in the realm? Do you realize the import of what I've become? You're as lost to me now as you were these last ten years."

"I don't believe that." Lizzie dipped the cloth into the water and slid it over his wounded shoulder first. "I cannot."

He ignored the slight burn, trapped in the torment of his conscience and his wants. He wanted Lizzie more than he wanted life. But how could he foist himself upon her when he would likely be dead before summer? He liked to think he was invincible, but the truth was that he'd lost too many brethren to mistake the reality of his profession.

She caressed a wet path over his chest and torso, then dipped the cloth back into the crock. His cock strained against his breeches. All it took was the slightest touch and he had no defenses against her.

"Why don't you believe that?" he asked, his voice thick. He was mesmerized.

She met his gaze, hers sultry and heavy-lidded. "Because I'm here with you. I'm yours, Edmond. I always have been. A woman's heart never lies."

He shouldn't press her further, he knew, but he couldn't resist. "And what does your heart say?"

Her nimble fingers went to his breeches and he almost lost his ability to think. "That I love you," she murmured.

Perhaps he was completely mad, he reasoned, because her

declaration made him harder still. "Lizzie, sweet." He should tell her how he felt, he knew, but he was frozen with the shock of her words. Though he'd braved death on many occasions, he was still terrified of the love he carried for her.

But Lizzie was hell-bent on torturing him. She opened the placket of his breeches, then came upon the bed to straddle him. His cock sprang free. She cast a wanton look his way before running the moist cloth over his rigid length. He groaned and thrust his hips. He wanted her berry-red mouth to replace the cloth.

As if hearing his silent plea, she closed her lips over his tip, sucking. It was all he could do to refrain from exploding in her mouth at the contact. There was something so tantalizing, so innocent and yet depraved about watching this good woman, still clothed in her sensible mantua, taking him into her mouth.

Her tongue flicked over him, and she took his cock deep into her throat. He moaned, sinking his fingers into her tight, wet heat. Lizzie sucked again, head moving up and down as she drew him into her throat, then out, then into the moist heat again. Within moments she brought him to shuddering release. Edmond watched as he pumped his seed into her open mouth. She met his gaze as she swallowed, then licked a teasing path across his cock.

The breath heaved from his lungs as he collapsed against the bed, spent and sated. Lizzie curled against him, rubbing his chest in soothing circles. He had never felt so loved. He wanted to return her generous words but somehow could not. In the end, he fell asleep with his woman's soft and reassuring form at his side.

THE NEXT MORNING was bright and sunny, the fright of the night's storm a thing of the past. Lizzie found Edmond on the quarterdeck, the wind ruffling his black hair. How she loved him, she thought, reveling in the sensation. It felt good to be free with him, to touch and kiss him as she wished. To indulge in all she had missed in the years she'd spent without him.

For however long it lasted. Her heart ached at the thought.

"Good morning," she greeted, pressing a kiss to his bearded cheek. His scent washed over her, a captivating blend of spice and sea air.

"Good morning, sweet Lizzie." He grinned, flashing a row of even teeth that were starkly white against his bronzed skin.

He was incredibly handsome, utterly captivating. Her heart swelled. Best to turn her mind to safer matters, she cautioned herself. She'd only make a cake of herself swooning all over him before his men.

She cast an admiring glance over the ocean surrounding them instead. "Why are we traveling so slowly?"

"We're limping," Edmond explained. "The storm forced us to turn south. We need to anchor and make some repairs."

"South?" She was startled by the revelation. "I thought we were headed north and I'd be returned to Philadelphia on your way back."

"Are you so eager to be rid of me, my dear?" His question was quick, cold.

"No," she answered truthfully, "but neither can I stay on a pirate's ship forever."

"Other women have before you," he responded in a thoughtful tone. "It's not unheard of."

Was he serious? Her heart leapt, ridiculous though his suggestion was. "Edmond, please don't speak of such things unless you are confident in what you say."

He reached for her hand, tangling his fingers with hers. "You know the more time I spend in your company, the more I want our idyll together never to end. But neither would I put you in danger. This is a hard life, Lizzie."

The familiar sadness crept through her again. She managed a smile, squeezing his hand. "We needn't make such decisions now. Where are we?"

"Just off Virginia," he responded, taking her cue and venturing once more into safer conversational waters. "We are well known here, which is both good and bad. The officials want us captured but the people have always been true to us. I'm hoping to go ashore for a few days, give Thomas the opportunity to regain his strength. We can't afford another storm or battle in the shape we're in."

"Very well. Can I be of service?" Lizzie doubted he'd allow her to perform labor of any sort, but she was feeling the need to be useful.

Edmond grinned. "You may watch us."

She sighed. "Am I never to have any adventure?" She had to admit she'd been secretly longing for excitement.

"I'm afraid not, my dear."

But just as he spoke the words, a cry sounded through the men. There was a ship approaching them, large and ominous on the horizon. Lizzie glanced back to Edmond, not missing the way he'd stiffened or the grim cast to his features.

"Other pirates?" she guessed.

"It's doubtful." He took her arm and began hauling her away from the sudden flurry of activity on the deck. "Whoever it may be, you'll have to go back down to the hold. It could be dangerous."

"Must I?" The thought of miserably awaiting her fate as she'd done during the storm was most unappealing to her.

"Yes. You must stay safe at all costs, Lizzie." He paused, naked emotion in his eyes. "I can't lose you."

It was the closest he'd come to an admission of tender feelings. Granted, potential peril loomed in the distance, but she took comfort in his confession nonetheless.

The ship was coming in at a good clip, spurred on by the wind and a number of men plying the oars. More cries rose from the pirates.

"I'll see myself below," she suggested. "Your men need you."

He nodded, his mind clearly wandering to the danger of the situation at hand. "Wait for me. I'll come to you."

Lizzie pretended to go below deck once more, but instead of following through with Edmond's dictates, she hid among some wine barrels that had been lashed together to survive the storm's angry waves. She took in the bustle of the pirates scurrying to their positions. Edmond ordered them to take up their muskets, and in the next few minutes, the details of the ship approaching them were delineated in the afternoon sunshine.

Dear God, the Royal Navy was upon them. Guns lined the ship that approached, its colors high, its menace sending ice into her soul. There was no way the pirates would be able to successfully defend themselves.

The fury of the evening's storm had taken its toll on the *Freedom*. Her mast had been severely damaged. Lizzie had seen the water she'd taken on in the hold as well. Now they were in no position to outmaneuver a frigate that appeared to outgun and outman them three to one.

Edmond gave the command to sail in an attempt at escape. But before they could make it far, the opposing ship unleashed the guns upon them. The jib halyard became the *Freedom's* first casualty, sending the foresails crashing down.

They instantly slowed, allowing their opponent the chance to draw nearer.

"Let them taste our musket fire," Edmond commanded over the confusion. "Send them to hell where they belong."

From her now-tenuous perch, she watched as Edmond gestured for his gunner to send a barrage of grapeshot toward the enemy. As the smoke cleared, the enemy ship was almost close enough to make out the features of its men. Edmond's pirates were faintly visible as they lit fuses in rum bottles and tossed them into the other ship. Explosions rocked the deck. The rum bottles, she realized, had been loaded with gunpowder, turning them into deadly weapons.

Her heart raced a mad pace as the opposing ship responded with another hail of gunfire. The sound of the battle was deafening, loud pops and cries mingling with the moans of wounded men. Even as the warfare unfolded, the *Freedom* was being guided to the shore. It appeared as if Edmond was attempting to run her aground to give his men a better chance. But suddenly, the enemy ship swung against the *Freedom*, the hulls of the two ships slamming together.

Edmond's men scurried aboard the other ship, swords drawn, facing off against the attacking ship's survivors. The clang of metal replaced the sound of gunfire. Lizzie was transfixed, frozen, horrified, unable to look away from the carnage. Good heavens, this was not the sort of adventure she'd had in mind. She frantically scanned the teeming throng of men in search of Edmond's beloved form. She found him facing off against the opposing ship's captain, who jumped aboard the *Freedom* in the melee.

Edmond thrust forward, engaging the other captain in a lightning-quick challenge of blades. As the two men fought, they moved slowly across the deck until they almost reached her hiding spot.

"I'd allow you to surrender," snarled the captain of the enemy ship, "but I'll enjoy killing you far more." He landed a glancing blow on Edmond's shoulder.

Lizzie held her breath. If she timed it properly, she believed she'd be capable of tripping Edmond's opponent. Their steps moved closer, as did the metallic clash of swords. Edmond's back was to her, his strong body tense as he fought for his life. His assailant was abreast of her in the next moment, completely unaware of her presence. She gauged her timing perfectly. Just as the captain took his next step, Lizzie slid her foot across his path.

He fell like a downed tree.

Chapter Nine

WHAT THE DEVIL? Edmond stared in shock at his opponent. He'd been about to deliver a death blow and now the bastard lay at his feet. Then he saw the innocent face of the woman he loved, who was not awaiting him in the hold as he'd requested.

Damn her. Pride in her bravery warred with anger for her carelessness. He didn't have time to deal with her recalcitrance but she'd get a tongue-lashing from him the instant this bloody battle came to an end.

He cuffed the captain on the back of the head with the butt of his gun. If the way the man's head thumped to the deck was any indication, he was unconscious. There was no help for it. He had to aid his men, which meant enlisting Lizzie, damn it all. He gave her his musket.

"Do you know how to shoot?" he shouted over clanging of cutlasses and the cries of the men.

"Yes, of course." She scrambled to hold the musket in its proper position. She looked awkard, but capable.

"Good. If he moves, kill him." He unsheathed his own cutlass. "By God, woman, don't leave this spot until I return."

Without waiting for her response, he rushed back into the skirmish. It was imperative they win this fight. As Edmond boarded the naval ship, he recognized the grisly carnage. Their gunner had done his work well. Men lay bloodied and battered across the deck. The *Freedom*, it seemed, would claim yet another ship.

Jean was in a heated session of swordplay, and Edmond rushed to his aid, cutting down the officer he fought from behind. Jean wiped blood from a cut on his cheek, grinning. "Thank you, Captain. These English puppies, they don't play fair."

"I'm an English puppy, if you'll recall."

"You're like me," Jean offered. "You have no country, Captain."

It was true. After all these years at sea, he truly felt he belonged nowhere and to no one. *Except Lizzie*, his heart reminded him. Edmond scanned the ship, sensing their enemies were ready to raise the white flag. "Drop your weapons! We'll be commanding this ship from now on, and if you value your life, surrender at once."

Arms clattered to the deck. The bloodied survivors of the battle were eager to save their own hides. Edmond appointed Jean in command of the naval ship and put ten of his men in charge of guarding prisoners before heading back to the *Freedom* and Lizzie.

To his surprise, she had listened to him. She was where he'd left her, presiding over the downed captain like an avenging pirate angel. A hot stab of lust went directly to his groin. *Sweet Christ*, he wanted her.

He loved her.

He never wanted to be without her. It was madness of the first order, but he didn't give a bloody damn. She was his. After all these years, they had found each other again. He would make it right between them. He had no other choice.

He took the musket from her. "Are you hurt?"

She appeared shaken by her first exposure to combat. She shook her head. "I am well. Are you unhurt, Edmond?"

"Always." He grinned with the triumph of the fight. "A little crew of navy puppies is no match for me."

Lizzie smiled halfheartedly, still clearly overwhelmed. "What shall we do with him?" She gestured to the captain.

"Fetch me some rope from over there," he told her. "We'll tie him up and make him sing."

If there was one thing he'd learned in his time on the sea, it was that with the proper incentive, naval officers liked to tell everything they knew. With the right amount of intimidation, he hoped the captain would reveal everything he knew about the state of things in the Chesapeake. He was beginning to feel like the fox in the hunt. He'd never been chased with as much determination as he had in these last few weeks. It was a grim sign that it may well be time to forego pirating for good.

When Lizzie returned with the rope as he'd asked, he lashed together the captain's hands and feet. It was time to uncover the truth and make a plan for the future, whatever it may bring.

LIZZIE WAS TIRED. It was all she could do to remain upright in her saddle. She felt as if she'd been riding forever. After burning the naval ship and sending it to the deep, they'd gone ashore. Edmond had learned through the captured captain that there were several ships and spies scouring the region in search of him. Governor Spotswood wanted his head more now than ever before. The news frightened Lizzie. She didn't much like the idea of being in close proximity to anyone who wanted to do Edmond harm.

She had reservations about throwing themselves upon the mercy of the people, but they had no other choice. Gunfire and the storm had rendered the *Freedom* thoroughly

SCARLETT SCOTT

compromised. So it was that with the few living prisoners gleaned from their opposing ship, they docked in Virginia and separated. The plan was set for all men to return within a week's time. Edmond had shared that he expected a week's time would provide enough opportunity to repair the ship and allow Thomas to recover properly.

Lizzie, Thomas and Edmond were on their way to a plantation owned by one of Edmond's friends. Because they only could obtain two horses, Edmond walked between Thomas and Lizzie. Fortunately, Thomas was able to sit a horse, but beyond that feat, he had little strength. He was still recuperating and weak.

"Are you sure this is wise?" she asked Edmond as they clopped through the dense forest.

"We have no choice, and the thinner we spread ourselves, the better," Edmond answered. "I've done this hundreds of times before. Have faith in me."

She did have faith in him, and yet she still harbored a niggling feeling in her stomach.

"I understand, Edmond, but I wish there was a better way." She prodded her roan along. He ever wanted to stop for a snack. Indeed, over the course of their hour's jaunt, he'd wanted to stop and relieve himself or eat at least half a dozen times.

"This is our only way, my love."

Suddenly, a disturbance rose in the undergrowth surrounding them. Lizzie saw the unmistakable blur of a man running, and in the next instant, shots were fired. She ducked low across the saddle as a musket ball sliced the air above her so close she could hear it. Dear God, for the second time in less than twenty-four hours, they were under attack.

"Lizzie," Edmond called, jumping up on the saddle behind Thomas, "ride east as hard as you can. Keep your head

74

down."

Terror clamped her heart like a fist. "What is happening?"

"Ride, Lizzie! We haven't much time."

Half a dozen men had emerged from the scrub, armed with muskets, all determined to capture or kill, whichever came first. Keeping her head down as Edmond had instructed, she kicked her roan into a gallop. The tepid creature was spooked by the gunfire and instantly tried to buck her. Lizzie held on, urging the horse to go faster. Suddenly her mount bucked again. She lost her tenuous grip on the reins and tried but failed to retrieve them. The roan reared up and the next thing she knew, Lizzie hurtled through the air.

Chapter Ten

SHE WOKE TO the throbbing of her head and utter confusion. *What in heaven's name?* She took in her surroundings: a small, sparsely decorated chamber, sunlight streaming in through a cracked window pane. Her hands were tied behind her back, her body thoroughly sore. She was seated in an unforgiving wooden chair.

Where was she? What had happened? Dozens of questions sifted through her mind.

The door to the chamber creaked open, revealing a man in officer's dress. She recognized him. Impossibly, he was the captain who had attacked Edmond's ship. He'd been left under Jean's guard, which meant that something was very much amiss.

It was then that comprehension hit her. She'd been captured. Fragments of her dash through the forest returned to her. She'd been pushing her mount, trying to escape, when the horse had thrown her.

Where was Edmond? What had happened to Jean?

"Ah, madam, I see you've decided to join us," the captain drawled with a sardonic air. "I trust you're comfortable?"

He enjoyed his power over her. She tipped up her chin, determined not to allow him to intimidate her. "Forgive me if I find your hospitality sadly lacking, sir."

"Such fire." He crossed the room, his booted footsteps

heavy, ominous. "It's little wonder he wanted you for himself."

Lizzie instinctively knew she could give no quarter to him. She feigned innocence. "Who are you speaking of, Captain?"

His eyes narrowed. "Don't play coy with me. I saw you with him aboard his ship with my own eyes."

"Of course I was aboard his ship. I was taken prisoner by him and his men." If she could just convince him she had nothing to do with Edmond, perhaps he would let her go.

"I think not." The captain lowered his face until she felt the heat of his breath fanning her lips. "I don't believe a word of what you've told me, madam. In fact, I believe you are that pirate bastard's whore."

She remained still, refusing to flinch or show even a pinch of fear. "I told you I was an innocent captive."

"You must think me a fool." He dragged his fingers over her cheek and she shrank from the touch. "What were you doing aboard his ship?"

"I was taken from a passenger ship," she repeated, holding her head high. She would not break. She would not allow him to see her faltering. "I expect the others drowned in the storm."

"Tripe." He gripped her arms with enough force to bruise. "If you won't tell me the truth, I'll be forced to make you."

Tears of pain stung her eyes but she refused to let them fall. Perhaps she needed to try another tactic. "The only tripe in this room is you, sir. How dare you treat a respectable lady in such a debased fashion? You ought to be ashamed of yourself. Does the governor know the depths to which his hired assassins have sunk? Preying on innocent women?"

He slapped her soundly across the face. "Where is he hiding?"

Shock rendered her numb for a few breaths. She realized he'd split her lip. The taste of blood tainted her tongue. There was a chance that if she didn't tell the captain something soon, he'd inflict far more pain upon her. He seemed determined to hunt down Edmond and he didn't have any compunction about abusing her to glean the information he sought.

"Maine," she said truthfully. "He said he was heading for Maine."

Of course, his path had changed dramatically given the storm and the battle. She had a feeling Maine was the last place he'd turn up at the moment, which was why she mentioned it so readily.

"He's on land now and Maine is out of the question. Surely he has a hideout here that you're aware of, madam."

Her gaze remained unwavering upon the captain's. "I am not privy to his hideouts, having just been his captive."

"Perhaps this will help you to think more clearly." He grabbed her curls, pulling her hair with a great deal of force.

Pain tore through her, sending tears to prick her eyes.

She feared he'd tear her hair from the roots even as she made an effort to remain outwardly stoic. "I cannot tell you what I don't know, Captain."

"Damn you," he growled, sending a spray of spittle over her face. "I'll have him at my mercy one way or another. You're only prolonging his inevitable hanging."

Her stomach was heavy as an anchor. "Honestly, sir, I don't have a care for the man. He was my captor, nothing more."

"Liar," he spat. "You were seen embracing him. You've been in his bed and there's no mistaking it."

"I'm a respectable widow," she maintained, hoping he couldn't sense her deception. She'd never been terribly good at prevarication. But if ever there was a need for it, surely it was this. If she remained impervious to the captain's abuses, she could at least give Edmond a fighting chance.

"I can see why he was so smitten with you that my men almost caught him." He released her hair and trailed the back of his hand down her throat. "Mayhap I should treat myself to your loveliness."

Instinct spurred her to action. She had to escape. With great effort to conceal her movement, she began testing her wrists against her bonds. They were loose enough that with sufficient wriggling she believed she could free herself. She needed to distract the captain long enough to accomplish the deed.

"Do you have a wife, Captain?"

Her question seemed to have the desired effect. He paused, his hand at her throat. "I fail to see that it's any business of yours."

Which meant he had a wife. She knew a surge of triumph before she dashed forward. "Imagine, for a moment, that your wife is on a passenger ship that was besieged by pirates. She's taken aboard the pirate vessel against her will. She's frightened and horridly mistreated." Behind her back, she slid her right hand free.

"My wife wouldn't cast herself into sin by giving herself to a pirate as you've done. And if she had, I'd hang her myself."

It was now or never, she realized, calling upon all the strength in her body. Lizzie had precious few choices. She lifted her legs and kicked against him with all her might. His response was instant. He stumbled back and Lizzie wasted no time in jumping from the chair. Her only option was to try running.

"Then I pity her, sir," she threw over her shoulder. And then, she threw open the door and ran directly into a man's solid chest.

EDMOND STAGGERED BACK, surprised by the female who had hurtled through the portal, nearly knocking him over in the process. He held her, anchoring her waist with his hands. "Steady."

He'd recognize those golden curls anywhere. Lizzie, thank hell. He drew her against him, breathing in her floral scent. Somehow, she always smelled of roses. He'd never forgive himself if something happened to her. She was all he'd been able to think of since they'd been separated.

Thankfully, he had some friends in the area who knew where Bertrand had taken up residence. He'd had a suspicion he would find her here.

"Edmond?" She looked up at him and he noticed a fine trail of blood on her lip. Someone had hurt her.

Bloodlust consumed him. He'd come to save her, and he could not leave her mistreatment unanswered. He stalked past her, hell-bent on pummeling the piss out of the bastard. Edmond caught him by his fancy jacket and threw him against the wall.

"You will never lay a hand on her again, Bertrand." His fist made a satisfying connection with the captain's face. "Never."

He swung again, but Bertrand was nimble. He side-stepped him and landed a jarring blow of his own in Edmond's eye. Edmond bloodied his nose. Bertrand pulled out a dagger.

"The governor has said the reward for you will be paid dead or alive," Bertrand taunted.

Edmond pulled a dagger from his boot, ready for hand-to-hand combat. He'd been in more than his fair share of knife fights, and he hadn't lost yet.

He feinted to the right and managed to slash Bertrand's sleeve. "Nothing would make me happier than giving you a scar to remember me by."

Bertrand sliced the top of Edmond's hand. He didn't even feel it, his body too numb. "I'll send you to hell, Grey," Bertrand snarled.

"Not if I send you first." Edmond raked Bertrand's side with his blade, then cut his hand so badly Bertrand dropped his dagger. Edmond kicked it across the floor to Lizzie.

Thank God he'd managed to recruit some of his men for the thorny task of rescuing Lizzie. Bertrand had rallied with his spies and mercenaries after escaping from his bindings and clubbing Jean over the head. It had taken Jean, Ollie and three others to subdue them before Edmond had even reached Lizzie. Now only one man remained. He circled Bertrand, wanting to kill the bastard.

"Edmond, don't!" It was Lizzie's voice that he heard above the rage pounding in his head, Lizzie's voice that made him stop.

He knew if he killed Bertrand, there would be no going back. And the truth of it was he didn't want to become beyond redemption in Lizzie's eyes. He didn't want to be a pirate whose only home was the sea. He wanted a wife, a life, a place where he was loved. He'd always known he couldn't be a pirate forever, and now there was a siren who called him louder than the ocean. Lizzie. His Lizzie.

He shoved Bertrand against the wall, pressing the tip of his blade into his skin with just enough force to release a bead of blood. "I could kill you now." He scored a fine scratch from left to right. "I could cut here, slit your throat."

"Please," Bertrand pleaded.

"But I won't." He gestured to Lizzie. "She has shown you mercy. Don't ever forget that."

Then he allowed his bitter enemy, the man who would have him dead, to walk away. It was, Edmond decided, his final act as a pirate. From this point forward, he was a new man.

Chapter Eleven

 FORTNIGHT LATER Lizzie was back aboard the *Freedom*. There was still a price on Edmond's head, but nevertheless, the crew had all reconvened unscathed. They had too many associates in the countryside to be found. They'd heard Bertrand had left Virginia to return to England, but it was likely that another vain glory seeker would take his place.

It seemed like her life for the last few weeks had been nothing but a dream. She'd almost come full circle. After spending time with some trusted friends of Edmond's, the crew was back aboard their intrepid ship, preparing to take sail.

Lizzie stood on the deck, the sun warming her back, content to watch Virginia slip away. She and Edmond had become inseparable. They were lovers and friends, and she hadn't pushed him for more. But sadness invaded her thoughts from time to time to think he would always belong to the sea, never to her.

"I want to show you something."

Lizzie jumped at the low rumble of Edmond's voice in her ear and spun to face him. "You scoundrel! You gave me quite a fright."

He smiled down at her, insufferably handsome as always. "I hope you'll forgive me when you see this." He extracted a sheet of paper from his coat. "This is for you, darling Lizzie."

Puzzled, she took the paper from him and unfolded it, reading the contents with dawning comprehension and a blossoming, frail sense of hope.

She nearly swooned from shock. "Edmond, is this real?"

He nodded, his smile turning into a smirk. "I've been granted a pardon by the governor. I'm a free man, no longer hunted, no longer above the law."

Her mind reeled. "How is this possible? He had a price on your head."

"I'm the Scourge of the Atlantic." He winked. "Nothing is impossible for me."

The rascal. Somehow he'd gained his freedom. He'd made it possible for them to have a future together. Dare she hope it meant he wanted her in his life forever? They'd been through so much in the last few days, and it had only served to strengthen their bond. And after their struggles, the pardon was a feat akin to a miracle.

"How did you really do it, Edmond?" Her curiosity wouldn't be deterred.

Edmond tucked a stray curl behind her ear. "I decided my run was over, and I had something the governor wanted while he had something I wanted. One of the first principles I learned as a pirate was the benefit of bartering."

He amazed her. "What did you barter?"

"A pardon for my assistance in bringing in the pirates who have been attacking the governor's shipping interests in the Chesapeake. Who better to catch a pirate than another pirate?" He shrugged. "It's simple. Fortunately, the governor saw the wisdom of my plan."

"That's wonderful." She threw her arms around his neck and dropped a kiss on his mouth. "Isn't it?" Doubts instantly pricked her mind. "Won't you miss the sea?"

He shook his head. "Not if I have you." He brought her

hands to his lips. "It's taken me ten years to find you again, and I'll be damned before I ever let you go. I'm sorry I ran from you, Lizzie. I've been to hell and back, and it's taken that for me to realize I'll never find myself without you. When we get to Philadelphia, I hope you will do me the honor of becoming my wife. I love you, Lizzie, more than pirating, more than the sea."

"Oh, Edmond." The tears rushing to her eyes blurred his beloved form. These were the words she'd longed to hear from him, the words she'd been too fearful to even hope for.

"What's this?" He caught a teardrop with his finger. "I hope I'm not so unsettling a future as all that."

"Of course not, you silly man." A bubble of ecstatic laughter burst inside her. "I've never been this happy in my life. I love you too, Edmond. I loved you when you were a boy, and I love you even more now that I see the man you've become."

He gazed down at her with so much tenderness it made her ache. "Marry me, my love?"

"Yes," she cried, tugging him to her for a passionate kiss. "A thousand times yes."

Epilogue

W HEN EDMOND DREAMT, it was of water. Brilliant and blue, the mindless lull of it rocking him in the night like a babe in a cradle. Or tossing and thrashing, in the midst of a violent storm. Some nights, the sea claimed him. Others, it tempted him. Powerful and vast, it was the only mistress he had ever known.

Until the mistress of his heart had returned to him, and he had realized love was more profound and precious than freedom, gold, and the sea combined.

In the bedchamber of their fine Virginia home, Edmond gazed fondly upon his wife, twin surges of desire and love uniting in an untamable deluge that threatened to drown him. It was a drowning he would gladly succumb to, if only it meant he could spend the rest of his days basking in her presence first.

What a beautiful bloody word that was, none finer in the English language: wife.

She smiled sleepily at him, her golden locks unbound and mussed about her shoulders, clad only in a robe that did little to conceal her ripe breasts, hard nipples, and the proud rounding of her belly. After too much time apart, he could not be more pleased to see his babe growing inside her. Indeed, the mere sight of her made his cock rigid.

"You are looking quite honorable these days, Mr. Grey,"

she teased softly, allowing her gaze to trail appreciatively over his fully clothed form.

He had a meeting with the governor today to discuss the addition of another ship in the Chesapeake to combat pirates, and he had dressed accordingly. He flashed her a rakish grin, unable to resist closing the distance between them. He was early for his meeting, was he not? And what sane man could leave his beautiful wife in such a state without doing something about it?

"Ah, my darling Lizzie, you should know me better than that by now. I may look honorable, but I'm afraid my intentions are decidedly the opposite." With his free hand, he drew apart her wrapper. "I can see your nipples through your night shift and I do not yet need to leave for my meeting. If you do not inform me otherwise, I'm going to strip you naked and suck them until you're wild for me."

They had been married for months, and still his words sent a flush of rose to her cheeks. "Is that a threat, or is it a promise, Captain Grey?"

He cupped her breasts, rubbing his thumbs over her taut nipples, gratified by her pleased moans. Now that she was with child, her body responded to his touch more eagerly than ever, and he could not deny himself every opportunity to pleasure her. "It is a promise, my love."

She shrugged out of her dressing gown, letting it fall to the floor in a whisper of sound. "Oh dear. My robe seems to have dropped, Captain. Whatever shall I do?"

Minx. He loved when she called him "Captain," and she knew it too well.

"I have an idea." He took her right hand in his, guiding her palm to where his cock strained against his breeches. "Or two…perhaps even three."

She caressed his rigid length boldly, just as she knew he

preferred. "Perhaps you ought to show me your ideas, husband. All three of them."

God's blood. The word "husband" in her sweet, husky voice broke the thin thread of his restraint. His hands found her waist, and he stepped nearer, her large belly brushing against him. Who needed dreams or a bloody ocean when he had this—*heaven*—in his arms? His mouth came down on hers in a ravenous kiss. His lips played over hers, opening for the warm slide of her tongue against his. She tasted sweet, like Lizzie, and earthy, like life and love and everything vital. He released her breasts and sank his fingers into her hair. Silky blonde waves tantalized him. He kissed her with the fever that had never stopped burning in his blood for her.

The fever that never would stop, not as long as he had breaths left to take.

He wanted her night shift gone, and so he rent it. The fortune he had amassed from his pirating days meant he could buy her a thousand more in its likeness and they would still never go hungry. She was naked, just as he preferred her to be, and his hands traveled. Over her swollen breasts, between her thighs. He dipped a finger into her folds, teasing her slick pearl. She moaned, straining against him, her tongue dueling with his.

He pulled away to drop open-mouthed kisses on her neck, then lower, to her breasts. When he sucked a pebbled nipple into his mouth, she jerked against him, whispering his name. His tongue raked over her nipple, toying with her, wanting her desperation to match his. She sank her fingers into his hair, tugging as she had learned he liked. He nipped her lightly with his teeth in reward until she moaned.

Edmond glanced up at her, feeling wicked. He tongued the nipple he'd just been torturing. "Do you like my mouth on you, Lizzie?"

"Oh yes," she whispered.

"Tell me what you want me to do."

Where once she would have hesitated, she had grown well accustomed to their love play.

"I want you to suck my other nipple," she murmured.

And he was grateful all over again for somehow finding her again. For making her his just as she always should have been. Just as she forever would be, in the same manner he was hers.

"With pleasure." He dipped his head and took the peak of the breast he'd ignored into his mouth. He sucked deeply, raked his teeth over her pretty, pink skin. His hands cupped the full undersides of both breasts, the signs of her body's preparation for bearing his babe leaving him awed and harder than ever all at once.

She rubbed her naked body against him, telling him without words just what she needed. He had made Lizzie into a wanton, and he did not regret a moment of debauching her.

He left her breast and dropped another kiss on her mouth. "Get on the edge of the bed."

She crossed the chamber and seated herself on the bed's edge, watching him approach her.

"Open your legs for me." He sank to his knees on the floor before her as though he were a courtier paying homage. And that was precisely what he was.

She parted her legs, and he feasted on the sight of her pale, curved thighs, her full belly, her mound and the glistening flesh at her core. He could not wait to taste her, and so he did not spare another moment more.

Edmond lowered his mouth to her, licking, playing his tongue over her, sucking, rubbing his beard over the sensitive flesh until she cried out. She arched into him, hungry for more. And he gladly gave it. His tongue sank inside her again and again until he could not wait another moment to be inside her.

He stood and removed his breeches. His fingers parted her folds, finding her passage slick and tight, gripping him. "You're so wet for me."

"I want you inside me, my love." She arched, moaning when a second finger joined the first.

He guided her legs so they rested on his chest, one on each of his shoulders. Then he lowered his hands to her waist, pulling her until her bottom was slightly off the bed's edge. He probed her entrance with the tip of his cock, playing with her, readying her. She jerked, and he plunged inside. Together, they began a delicious rhythm. Again and again he sank inside her, then drew almost out entirely, then deep once more. She cried out as a spasm overcame her and she reached her pinnacle. He continued, increasing his thrusts in speed and strength, and he was so deep inside her. So deep, and so lost, and so in love. The sea could not compare to Lizzie Grey.

In a few more deep strokes, she came again as he pumped his seed inside her, thrusting and rotating his hips. Liquid warmth shot through him. His moan mingled with hers. Neither of them moved for a few beats of the heart, savoring the aftermath of their frenzied loving.

Finally, he withdrew from her and fell to the bed at her side, lying on his back. Naked, sated, and glorious as any goddess, she curled against him, nestling her head onto his shoulder. Her hand rested above his galloping heart.

"Do you remember the first time we met, my love?" she asked.

It was a day he would never forget.

He smiled, laying his hand over hers, lacing their fingers together. "You wore a simple black gown, and I mistook you for a servant, but you were the loveliest thing I had ever seen. I wanted to make you mine even though I knew I never could."

"But you did, and I will be forever thankful for that day." She pressed a kiss to his jaw. "Did you know the cakes were not well received? One was dry, and the other too moist. My father insisted I choose a different baker, and I lied to him and told him that I had. I was desperate for any reason to see you again."

He was sated, happier than he had ever dreamed he could be, and desperately in love. This—here, in Lizzie's bed and in her arms, their babe growing in her womb—was where he was meant to be. Not the ocean. Not aboard a ship. But with this brave, valiant, intelligent, giving woman who made him whole.

"I was never any bloody good at being a baker," he said with a grin, turning to fuse their lips in another long, deep kiss. "But I do hope I make a good husband to you, and a good father to our babes." His hand cradled her stomach reverently. He could never touch her there enough, it seemed. Life could confound, bit it could also astound in the most majestic manners.

"You are the best husband, my darling man," she said softly, love shining brilliantly in her eyes as she cupped his cheek. "And you will make the best father as well. This I know. I love you."

"I love you more than you can possibly know." He could not resist kissing her once more. And then again. And again. And…well, damn his blood, the governor could wait.

THE END.

Dear Reader

Thank you for reading Edmond and Lizzie's story! Their happily ever after was filled with adventure and peril, but in the end, true love conquered all just as it should. If you're looking for equally thrilling reads filled with passion and intrigue, do read on for excerpts from the League of Dukes series.

Until next time,

Scarlett

Nobody's Duke

League of Dukes Book 1

By
SCARLETT SCOTT

A widow with secrets

When the dangerous men who killed her husband in a political assassination threaten Ara, Duchess of Burghly, the Crown assigns her a bodyguard. But the man charged with protecting her is no stranger.

He's Clayton Ludlow, the bastard son of a duke and the first man she ever loved. Eight years after he took her innocence and ruthlessly abandoned her, he's back in her drawing room and her life.

This time, she's older, wiser, and stronger. She will resist him at any cost and make him pay for the past.

A man with a broken heart

She's the only woman Clay ever loved and the one he hates above all others. When Ara brutally betrayed and deceived him, leaving him with a scarred face and a bitter heart, he devoted himself to earning his reputation as one of the Crown's most feared agents.

He wants nothing more than to finish his assignment so that he can remove all traces of her from his life forever. But walking away from her for good won't be as easy as he thinks.

As secrets are revealed and danger threatens Ara, Clay discovers that the truth is far more complicated than deceit. Once she's back in his arms where she belongs, he'll wage the biggest fight of all to keep her there.

Chapter One

London, 1882

𝒯O SOCIETY, SHE was the Duchess of Burghly. To her husband, murdered by a Fenian's blade, she had been Araminta, formal and proper and beloved by him in his way. She had loved him equally in her way. Sweet Freddie, with the heart of an angel and the desire to change a world that would never understand or accept him.

She was all too familiar with the way the world treated hopeful, unsullied hearts.

"Ara."

She had been hopeful and unsullied once.

When she had known the man standing before her in the drawing room of Burghly House. When she had loved him. When she had been…

"Ara."

There it was again, spoken with such dark vehemence that it almost vibrated in the air, sending unwanted tendrils of heat licking through her even after all the years that had passed. That name, that bitter reminder of who she had been, spoken in the voice that had once sent a thrill straight to her heart…it was her undoing.

Ara had not realized she had clambered to her feet until her body swayed like a tree caught in an aggressive wind. Faintness overcame her. Her vision darkened. The palms clenching her silken skirts were damp, hands trembling.

He was taller than she remembered. Broader and stronger.

He had always been a mountain of a man, but he had grown into his bones and skin, and the result took her breath despite her fierce need to remain as unaffected by him as possible. His eyes, cold and flat, burned into her. His jaw was rigid, his expression blank. A vicious-looking scar cut down his cheek.

She wondered for a moment how he could have received such a mark.

And then she reminded herself that she did not care. That he had ceased to be someone she worried after some eight years ago, on the day she had waited for him with nothing more than a valise and her foolish heart. He had never come.

The agony of that day returned to her a hundredfold as she stood in the gilt splendor of her drawing room, stabbing at her with the precision of a blade. Hours had passed, day bleeding into evening, and she had waited and waited. The only carriage to arrive had been her father's, and it had taken her, broken and dejected, back to the place from which she had fled.

"Your Grace, are you well?"

The voice of the Duke of Carlisle, edged with concern, pierced her consciousness, reminding her she had an audience, lest she allow her dignity to so diminish that she allowed *him* to see the visceral effect he had upon her.

She swallowed, tamped down the bile threatening to curdle her throat, and turned her attention to Carlisle. "I am as well as can be expected, given the events of the last three months, Duke. I thank you for your concern."

He inclined his head. "I am deeply sorry for the loss of your husband, madam. He was a bright star in the Liberal party."

"Yes," she agreed, a tremor in her voice that she could not suppress. Speaking of Freddie inevitably festered a resurgence of horror and sadness. He had been a good man, an estimable husband to her and father to Edward, and he had not deserved to die choking on his own blood in a Dublin park. "He was."

Carlisle's lips compressed into a pained frown. "I cannot begin to fathom your grief, and I apologize for our unwanted presence here today. If there were any way to keep you free of this burden, I wholeheartedly would."

"The grief is immense," she whispered, all she could manage past the knot in her throat.

How she hated that it wasn't just her sorrow for Freddie that paralyzed her now and stole her voice. She felt *his* stare upon her like a brand. He had not moved. Had not spoken another word save her name, and yet he seemed to have stolen all the air from the room.

"As I was saying prior to Mr. Ludlow's arrival," Carlisle continued with a formal tone, "it is with great regret that I find myself tasked with informing you that there has been a threat made against you by the same faction of Fenians that murdered your husband. To that end, the Home Office has assigned an agent to ensure your protection."

Carlisle's words sank into her mind as though spoken from a great distance.

…a threat made against you…

…same Fenians that murdered…

…an agent to ensure your protection.

Her breathing was shallow. Her fingers fisted in her skirts with so much force that her knuckles ached. Still, the weight of *his* burning gaze upon her would not lift. Her entire body felt achy and hot and itchy and chaotic all at once.

"Would you care to elaborate on the nature of the threat?" She kept her eyes carefully trained upon the Duke of Carlisle, but it was impossible to keep *him* from her peripheral vision. He filled the chamber as much with his presence as with his massive size.

The Duke of Carlisle, despite his reputation as a depraved reprobate, was the unexpected liaison between herself and the department of the government responsible for informing her about Freddie's murder and the investigation into finding his assassins. Their previous meetings had been equally stilted, revolving around his sympathy for her loss and any new information regarding the Fenians who had plotted Freddie's death.

In the murky days following her husband's murder, she and Edward had been removed from Dublin with an armed escort, but she had imagined that they had left all danger behind them in Ireland.

"Assassination, Your Grace." Carlisle's tone was quiet but deadly serious.

Those three words, so succinct and cold, struck her heart.

Edward could not lose both his parents in the span of three months. Her heart squeezed at the thought of her son alone in the world. Her beautiful, kindhearted boy. She would do anything to protect him.

Her mouth went dry. "I see." She paused, attempted to collect herself, an odd mixture of discomfit at *his* continued presence and fear swirling through her. "My son, Your Grace? Has he been included in the threats as well, or do they only pertain to myself?"

"Your son was not referenced in the threats, Your Grace," Carlisle said.

"*You have a son?*"

She flinched, the angry lash of *his* voice striking her. Still, she would not look at *him*. "I do not understand the reason for your…associate's presence, Your Grace. Indeed, I would far prefer to conduct this dialogue with you in private, as befitting the sensitive nature of the circumstances."

Ara refused to say *his* name. Refused to even think it.

Would not speak aloud the true nature of what and who he was. A bastard. The half brother of the Duke of Carlisle. The man she had lost her heart and her innocence to. Her son's father.

No. Freddie had been Edward's father, the only one he had ever known. And it must—*would*—remain that way until she went to her grave.

The Duke of Carlisle appeared unperturbed by her uncharacteristic outburst. "Pray forgive me again, Duchess, but Mr. Ludlow's presence here today is necessary as he is the agent who has been assigned to your protection."

"No!" The word left her in a cry, torn from her, vehement.

But what surprised her the most was that it was echoed by another voice, dark and deep and haunting in its velvety timbre.

His.

Her gaze flitted back to him, and the stark rage she read reflected in the depths of his brown eyes shook her. Beneath the surface, he was seething.

"I will not guard her under any circumstances, Leo. Find someone else," he sneered. "Anyone else."

And then he turned on his heel and stalked from her drawing room, slamming the door at his back.

CLAY'S FEET COULD not carry him far enough or fast enough away. *Damn it all to hell.* Damn Leo to hell. But most of all, damn *her.* Time and distance were not panaceas, but they had been his sole comfort, and now even that would be stolen from him if he allowed it.

He could not allow that. She had broken him once. Never

again.

The urge to strike something or someone—to smite and thrash with a violent savagery borne of all the fury flashing inside him—had never been stronger. Eight years and she had not changed. If anything, she had grown more ethereal. She had always been lovely, with her pale skin and coppery curls, the blue-violet eyes framed by long, dark lashes that stared at a man as if they could see into the dark pit of his soul.

Ara, his Ara.

No. Not my Ara.

Not any longer.

Nothing had made that clearer than the day she had confessed to her father that the Duke of Carlisle's bastard son had taken her innocence. He could feel the blade of the knife slashing his cheek as if it were yesterday. Could still smell the fetid breath of the man who had marked him for life. His scar ached and burned, a permanent, visceral reminder of why he could not even breathe the same air as the woman he had just turned his back upon.

"Clay."

The commanding sound of his half brother's voice halted him, but his cessation of movement was an act of duty and nothing less. If he had his way, he would be halfway across London by now, putting as much distance as possible between himself and the woman he had once loved.

Fists clenched, he spun around. As tall and dark as Clay though not as broad, Leo had nabbed the fortune of being born on the right side of the blanket, which upon their sire's death several years prior had made him the rightful duke. Though he was three months Clay's junior, he was also his superior in the clandestine ranks that had been created by the Home Office known simply as the Special League.

Those twin facts would always rankle.

He waited for Leo to approach him, trying to temper his rage.

"Where the hell do you think you are going?" Leo demanded without preamble, irritation twisting his countenance and rendering it even grimmer than it ordinarily was.

Calm yourself, Clay. She can likely hear everything from where she waits in her gilded little drawing room. Do not give her the pleasure of knowing how much the sight of her affects you after all these years. You can never again allow her to see your weakness.

"I respectfully request to be assigned elsewhere," he clipped.

Leo did not miss a beat. "No."

He resisted the urge to roar or slam his fist into his brother's face. "Allow me to rephrase. I am not requesting. I am demanding."

Leo flashed him a small, severe smile. "Once again, no."

"I cannot guard her." The low confession was torn from him.

He did not want to admit it. Not aloud and especially not to his brother, who traded in the weaknesses of others. Blood they may share, but Leo did not yield for anyone. He had inherited his mother's icy temperament and sternness, where Clay had his own mother's soft, giving heart.

Or at least he had, once.

"You can and you must," Leo insisted. "You are aware of what happened to the duchess's husband."

The Duke of Burghly, the Chief Secretary for Ireland, had been stabbed to death in a Dublin park in the midst of a spring afternoon, along with his undersecretary. They had been beset by men wielding surgical knives, all the better to inflict deathblows. Whilst the men responsible for the outrage had escaped, evidence pointed in one direction only: the

Fenians.

"Of course I am bloody well aware, Leo," he said, fists and jaw still equally clenched. "But that has no bearing upon my presence here in her home. I cannot—will not remain here. The League is rife with other agents. Choose another one."

"No one else is you, Clay. You can and will accept this post and guard her, because you must." Leo paused, lowering his voice. "I know the two of you share a past, but I had not realized you still have feelings for her."

"I don't," he denied with force. Too much force.

He had feelings for her, in truth. Loathing. Anger. Rage. Betrayal. Those were the sorts of emotions she had left behind along with the scar. And just like the mark upon his flesh, they would disfigure him for his lifetime.

"Then there is no reason why you cannot accept the position." Leo's tone smacked of finality.

Yes, damn it. There was *every* reason.

"I cannot be in proximity to her, Leo." There, he admitted it. Just seeing her had shaken him. If he had known she had become the Duchess of Burghly, he never would have even deigned to come to Burghly House at all. She was like a broken rib, hurting him with each breath, a danger to his lungs. "You deliberately misled me in bringing me here."

"I did not mislead you," his brother argued, keeping his voice quiet so it would not carry back to the drawing room. "I acted in the best interest of the Home Office, the Special League, and the duchess. You must consider the matter rationally, Clay, and not with your heart."

"I am being as bloody rational as I can be when it pertains to that woman," he growled. "My heart has naught to do with it, of that I can assure you. My patience, however, my anger, my sanity…those things cannot withstand being in her presence for longer than I have already endured."

Leo remained unmoved. "We cannot afford to allow the Fenians to claim another victim. The assassination of a duchess here on English soil, coupled with the bombings we have endured and foiled, would spark fear and pandemonium."

An assassination.

Ara's assassination.

Her *murder*.

The sobering thoughts chased the heat of his rage, replacing it with a numbing chill. As much as he loathed not just the sight of her but everything she had done to him—her betrayal and her willingness to toss him away like an outmoded gown—the notion of her meeting her end in the same gory fashion as the duke made bile churn in his gut. The threats made against her were not just real; they were possible. The Fenians wanted Irish home rule, and they were not above terrorizing, bombing, and killing anyone they imagined stood in the way of their cause in an effort to gain it.

An ingenious part of their evil strategy was to bring war to England without ever sending an army. Small groups of plotters had already invaded towns and ports. A bomb last year in Salford had killed a young boy when it exploded. Other bombs had exploded in Liverpool, and various plots had been uncovered and stopped throughout London.

Now they had begun a different prong of attack, targeting government officials like the Duke of Burghly. And like his widowed duchess. Ara was being threatened by the most ruthless, fearless, and dangerous sort of men: those who perceived they had nothing left to lose.

But even so, she was not his responsibility. She had ceased being his *anything* the day she had chosen to destroy him. He would not save her. The burden was too great for him to bear.

He shook his head. "I am sorry, Leo, but any other

SCARLETT SCOTT

League member is as suited as I am for the role, if not more so. I cannot pretend I would be able to maintain indifference and guard her as will be necessary. Forcing me to do this is both unwise and dangerous to the lady, who is deserving of the basic right of safety, no better or worse than any other person."

"No one is as suited as you, Clay." His brother's dark gaze was unrelenting. "You have thwarted dozens of assassination attempts. Your work protecting the Duchess of Leeds was commendable, and you had no problems settling yourself into a more domestic setting than you have been previously accustomed."

The Duchess of Leeds had been the victim of a murderous plot, and he had served her well. In so doing, she had become his friend. She possessed the heart of an angel, with a willingness to take in all the stray beasts of London, but she had been different. She had not been Ara.

He had never loved her.

And it did not matter how much time had passed. He had not forgotten a moment of the time he had spent with Ara. Kissing her, holding her, the wildness of her burnished curls tangling around them. The soft giggles he could coax from her lips with his wandering mouth and hands.

He shook himself free of the memories, cloying like ivy, threatening to choke and overrun him. "My history with her renders it an impossibility. What of Strathmore? He would be an excellent man for the job."

"He is otherwise occupied," Leo said curtly. "I grow weary of your objections, brother, as they are all immaterial at worst and flimsy at best. You are the man I have chosen, the man the Home Office has chosen, to protect her."

"I don't give a damn," he thundered as the last, fine filament of his control broke. "I will not do it."

"Sodding hell, Clay." His brother fixed a dispassionate frown upon him. "I did not wish to do this, but you have left me without a choice. If you do not take on this task, you will be suspended from service. The Home Office requires you to perform this duty, and they will not accept anyone else. Do you not think I already tried to substitute another, knowing of your past?"

His heart thrummed faster, his chest rising and falling, each breath harsher than the next. He had never supposed Leo would attempt to protect him in such a fashion. Though they had come of age side by side, Leo possessed not a modicum of maudlin sentiment, or so Clay had always supposed.

"Suspended from service," he bit out, as though the words tasted bitter and ugly in his mouth. For they did. His work in the Special League was what had given him purpose these last eight years. Because of her, it was all he had. And now because of her, he also stood to lose it.

How bloody fitting.

"I am sorry, brother." Leo's somber tone said more than his apology could convey.

He swallowed the bile that had begun in his stomach and worked its way into his throat. "I do not have a choice, do I?"

Leo's lips compressed. "I am afraid not."

He spun away, stalking down the hall, intent upon inflicting damage upon the first inanimate object he spied. With his fists. But there was nothing in sight that he could punch, aside from damask-covered walls and tables rife with bric-a-brac. Pictures of her. Pictures of her husband. Of the two of them with a small lad.

He could not face them, so he turned back to the fate awaiting him. His life had never been his to rule. Why should this assignment be any different? He would do what he must. Because there was no other option.

"Very well. I shall do it." He gave a terse nod, feeling a heavy weight descend upon his chest as he acquiesced. It held the finality of a death sentence, and he had never felt more like a man being informed of his impending swing upon the gallows.

"Good man." Leo strode to him and clapped him on the shoulder. "I know what this is costing you, Clay, and do not think that I don't appreciate it. I will continue to assert pressure for you regarding the creation of a peerage."

Following his previous assignment, there had been rumbles that he may be rewarded for his service to the Crown with a title. Clay knew better than to hope for such an eventuality.

"Do you think I give a damn about gaining a title?" he asked dismissively, his lip curling. "I never have, and I never will."

But that was a lie, and he knew it. For if he had possessed a title, he would still have Ara. He never would have lost her.

"Even so," Leo said, "you deserve recompense for your service. There is no man better."

"I am doing this because I must and for no other reason," he persisted. "But I do not like it, Leo. And neither will I forget it."

His half brother gave him an odd little smile then. "Let it be just one more to add to the vast catalog of black marks upon my soul."

Clay could only hope it would not also be a black mark upon his.

Exclusive Bonus Teaser from League of Dukes Book 2, *Heartless Duke*!

Prologue

Oxfordshire, 1882

THE DUKE OF Carlisle landed at his half brother's estate in Oxfordshire with a small cadre of servants and one armed guard, dusty, travel-worn, and weary. It seemed wrong somehow to arrive at Clay's wedding after having spent the previous night surrounded by the most depraved and licentious acts imaginable.

Or at least those imaginable to Leo, and his mind was blessed with a boundless creativity for the wicked.

But here he was, prepared to do his duty.

Duty was everything to him, for it was all he bloody well had.

He was also late, the hour approaching midnight, but he had allowed himself to be distracted at a tavern blessedly in possession of a hearty store of spirits. It was possible that he was drunk as well, having consumed roughly enough ale and wine to float the Spanish Armada.

A poor decision, that. He ought to have arrived earlier like a gentleman.

He flung open his carriage door and leapt down without

waiting for it to reach a complete stop. Fortunately, he was blessed with a cat's stealthy reflexes even when bosky, and he landed in the gravel on two booted feet with effortless grace.

Farleigh, one of the men standing guard over Harlton Hall whilst his brother's wife-to-be continued to be in danger, approached him first. The political assassination of her husband had left her a target for a particularly ruthless ring of Fenians.

An unfortunate business, indeed. One Leo was doing his utmost to rectify. The criminals would be brought to justice by his hand, one way or another. Death just as swift a sentence as prison. He would choose death for the miscreants over imprisonment every time.

"Your Grace," Farleigh said, bowing. "You ought to take better care. You could have been injured."

Leo flicked a cold gaze over the man. "Yet, I was not. Is the entire household abed, sir?"

"There are some who have awaited your arrival. They will see to it that your belongings are taken to the proper chamber and you are settled."

Leo's lips thinned. Apathy, as vast as it had ever been, was a chasm inside his chest, threatening to consume him. Likely, he ought to find his chamber, order a bath, and scrub himself clean of the stink of London and the road.

But all he truly wanted was more liquor and some distraction, not necessarily—but preferably—in that order.

"Have there been any incidents since the relocation from London?" he asked sharply.

Even in his cups, he could not shake himself of the burden of his duties. He was the leader of the secretive branch of the Home Office known as the Special League. The safety and wellbeing of England's citizenry was in his hands. And the plague of the Fenian menace was evidenced everywhere these days: bombs exploding across England, vicious murders carried out, all in the name of Irish nationalism.

Some days, he needed to over imbibe.

He allowed such a weakness once per month, no more.

"There have been none, Your Grace," Farleigh confirmed. "The decision to leave town and come here with Her Grace was a wise one."

"Of course it was," Leo drawled. "I made it."

Aware of his rudeness and not giving a good goddamn, Leo stalked past Farleigh, his long legs taking him up the stairs leading to Harlton Hall. He did not bother himself with the details of his trunks or even which chamber had been assigned him. Instead, he went in search of his quarry.

Whisky. Brandy. Ale. *Holy hell*, even Madeira would do at the moment, and he disliked it intensely. He was in a foul mood, and he did not know why, other than that the Fenians continued to outmaneuver him.

No one outmaneuvered the Duke of Carlisle, by God.

He stalked through the entry and main hall, and was about to acknowledge defeat when he strode into a darkened chamber and collided with something soft. Something feminine and deliciously scented. *Ah, lemon and bergamot oil.* Something—his hands discovered a well-curved waist—or rather *someone.*

"I beg your pardon," the lady said with a huff and the slightest lilt to her accent he could not place.

"You may, but perhaps I shall not grant it," he said, feeling like the devil tonight.

"Grant what, sir?"

"My pardon." He dipped his head lower, drawn to her warmth. Though he could see only faint outlines of her as his eyes adjusted to the dim light—a cloud of dark hair, a small, retroussé nose, a stubborn chin—he was nevertheless drawn to her. "Have you done something requiring it?"

She made a sound of irritation in her throat. "Release me, if you please. I have neither the time nor the inclination to play games with a stranger who arrives in the midst of the night, smelling of spirits."

"Allow me to introduce myself." He stepped back, offering her an exaggerated bow. "The Duke of Carlisle, m'lady. And you are?"

She moved forward, into the soft light of the hall. With the gas lamps illuminating her fully at last, he felt as if he had received a fist to the gut. She was striking, from her almost midnight hair, to her arresting blue gaze, to the full pout of her pink lips. And she was proportioned just as he preferred: short of stature yet shapely. Her bosom jutted forward in her plain dove-gray bodice.

Damn him if the woman wasn't giving him a cockstand here and now, at midnight in the midst of the hall with the hushed sound of servants seeing to his cases fluttering around them. They were not alone, and yet they might have been the only two souls in the world.

Her eyes sparkled with intelligence, and he could not shake the feeling that she was assessing him somehow. "I serve as governess to the young duke."

Governess.

That explained the godawful gray gown.

It did not, however, explain his inconvenient and thoroughly unwanted attraction to her. He did not dally with servants.

More's the pity.

Leo frowned. "What is the governess doing flitting about in the midst of the night, trading barbs with a stranger who smells of spirits?"

He could not resist goading her, it was true.

Her brows snapped together. "You waylaid me, Your Grace."

He would love to waylay her. All bloody night long.

But such mischief was decidedly not on the menu for this evening. Or ever. He had far too many matters weighing on his mind, and the last thing he needed to do was ruin a governess. He had come to celebrate his brother's nuptials, *damn it*, not to cast the last shred of his honor into the wind.

"Whilst you are being waylaid, perhaps you can direct me to the library," he said then. "I am in need of diversion. My mind does not do well with travel."

The truth was that his mind was not well in general, and it hadn't a thing to do with trains and coaches. But that was his private concern, yet another weakness he would admit to no one.

He expected the woman to inform him which chamber he sought and how he might arrive there. He did not expect her frown to deepen, or for her to turn on her heel and stride away down the hall in the opposite direction.

"Follow me, if you please," she called over her shoulder. "I shall take you there."

Leo followed, admiring the delectable sway of her hips as they went.

The governess intrigued him far too much, and he hoped to hell it wasn't going to become a problem. As it stood, he would only be at Harlton Hall for a few days' time. What could possibly go wrong?

A whole bloody lot, answered a voice inside him.

He ignored it. A faint hint of lemon taunted him. Nor could he wrest his gaze from her. She was exquisitely formed. *And a governess*, he reminded himself. When had he last been intrigued by a female? It had been years. It had been Jane, to be precise. Her name still curdled his gut, even after all the summers and winters since she had married Ashelford. That had been when Leo had been a callow youth still foolish enough to believe a woman's heart could be steadfast. Good of her to rectify his ignorance. His allegiance belonged to the League now and forever, just as it always should have done. Crown and country. The safety of England.

Not the tempting swell of the governess's lower lip. So full and bewitching, that succulent pink flesh. He longed to sink his teeth into it. The spirits he had consumed were making him maudlin and randy in equal measures, he decided as they entered a long, narrow chamber with shelf-lined walls. A bloody terrible, dreadful coupling. He required more liquor at once, for nothing blunted the furious grip of lust like the obliteration to be found at the bottom of a bottle.

The gas lamps were low, bathing the room in a soft sensibility that did nothing to alleviate the inappropriate bent of his meandering thoughts. His brother had yet to fill the shelves. The books were scarce, though the carpet was new, and a banked fire crackled in the hearth.

She stopped on the periphery of the chamber, spinning toward him, hands laced together at her waist. He noted the bones of her knuckles, white through her skin. Her shoulders were stiff, her neck rigid, entire body immobile, almost as though she stood on a slippery slope and didn't wish to move lest she go tumbling down.

Leo was trained to observe. He trusted no one but his brother Clay and the woman he considered his true mother. Everyone else was suspect. What could a pretty little governess like her have to hide? What did she fear?

He moved nearer to her, driven by suspicion. Driven by need. Driven by the darkness inside him. By desire. Today, he could not rein himself in. He stopped just short of her, crowding her with his considerable height. She scarcely

EXCERPT FROM HEARTLESS DUKE

reached his shoulder.

The deeper note of bergamot hit him. Her eyes widened. They were not pure blue. Flecks of gray enriched them. Her brows were fine and dark, elegantly arched. A flush stole over her cheeks at his silent regard.

"Here we are, Your Grace," she said softly. Her voice was husky. It was like a plume of fine cigar smoke, unfurling to envelop him. "The library, just as you requested."

She remained so still and tense. A doe in the wood poised for flight. Was he the hunter, arrow nocked? He was too intrigued to step away. Too intrigued even to search for more spirits. Surely Clay had whisky, and he would find it at his leisure. First, there was something about this blasted governess. Something he could not shake.

"Your name." He meant to ask her a question, but he was not terribly adept at polite conversation. He led his agents. He hosted depraved fetes at his townhouse. He did not speak to governesses, pay social calls, or whirl about at balls. He was a machine. And like any machine, he was beginning to show wear.

"Palliser, Your Grace."

"Miss Palliser," he repeated, thinking the name familiar. He searched the dusty corners of his mind before lighting upon it. "Glencora, by any chance?"

It was meant to be a sally, a reference to the Anthony Trollope character—an irregularity for him, as he had not much cause for levity in his life—but the governess paled, her lips parting. "Jane Palliser, Your Grace."

Christ. There was that hated name again. Surely, this was the Lord's idea of a cruel jest. A means of retribution for the vast catalog of sins Leo had committed in the name of serving his queen. Why else would a governess with the face of an angel and the body of a courtesan be placed before him on this day of weakness, bearing the same name as the woman who had nearly been his ruin?

His lip curled. "Jane." The name felt heavy on his tongue, acidic and bitter, the taste of disillusionment, and even though this was a different Jane before him, he could not separate the emotions from the moment. "You do not look like a Jane to me."

Her eyes widened almost imperceptibly. "And yet, that is what my mother chose to name me, Your Grace. I am so sorry to disappoint you."

He did not miss the undercurrent in her voice, a strange hint of something that suggested Miss Jane Palliser harbored secrets. Perhaps he would make it his mission to uncover them during his brief stay at Harlton Hall.

Leo raked his gaze over her in an assessing fashion, unable to resist the urge to discomfit her. "I doubt you could disappoint me, Miss Palliser."

THE DUKE OF Carlisle had come to Harlton Hall. It was almost not to be believed, far too fortuitous a circumstance to be ascribed to anything other than fate. And he was not just here, within her presence, within her reach, standing near enough to touch in the barren library, but he was *flirting*. With her, or at least with the woman he presumed her to be. Pretty London lass Jane Palliser. Nothing but a fiction.

The anxiety she had known upon his sudden proximity and odd queries—the dark, plumbing gaze of his that seemed to see far more than she wished, cutting straight to the heart of all her desperate prevarications—lifted. She was accustomed to men who thought they could have everything they wanted. She had spent her life in their shadows.

She gritted her teeth and forced herself not to allow her hatred to show. He wanted her, and if there was one thing she had learned in her life, it was the power a woman wielded over a man. One twitch of her skirts, the revelation of an ankle, the flit of her tongue over her lips, and he would be in the palm of her hand.

Precisely where she wished him.

For she may have arrived at Harlton Hall as Miss Jane Palliser, but in truth, she was Bridget O'Malley, and she had come to fight a war.

Want more? Get *Heartless Duke*!

Don't miss Scarlett's other romances!

(Listed by Series)

HISTORICAL ROMANCE

Heart's Temptation
A Mad Passion (Book One)
Rebel Love (Book Two)
Reckless Need (Book Three)
Sweet Scandal (Book Four)
Restless Rake (Book Five)
Darling Duke (Book Six)

Wicked Husbands
Her Errant Earl (Book One)
Her Lovestruck Lord (Book Two)
Her Reformed Rake (Book Three)
Her Deceptive Duke (Book Four)

League of Dukes
Nobody's Duke (Book One)
Heartless Duke (Book Two)

Sins and Scoundrels
Duke of Depravity (Book One)

Stand-alone Novella
Lord of Pirates

CONTEMPORARY ROMANCE

Love's Second Chance
Reprieve (Book One)
Perfect Persuasion (Book Two)
Win My Love (Book Three)

Coastal Heat
Loved Up (Book One)

About the Author

Amazon bestselling author Scarlett Scott writes steamy Victorian and Regency romance with strong, intelligent heroines and sexy alpha heroes. She lives in Pennsylvania with her Canadian husband, adorable identical twins, and one TV-loving dog.

A self-professed literary junkie and nerd, she loves reading anything, but especially romance novels, poetry, and Middle English verse. When she's not reading, writing, wrangling kids, or indulging in her inappropriate sense of humor, you can catch up with her on her website www.scarlettscottauthor.com. Hearing from readers never fails to make her day.

Scarlett's complete book list and information about upcoming releases can be found at www.scarlettscottauthor.com.

Connect with Scarlett! You can find her here:
Join Scarlett Scott's reader's group on Facebook for exclusive excerpts of works in progress, cover reveals, takeovers, tons of giveaways, and a whole lot of fun with likeminded people!
facebook.com/groups/scarlettscottreaders
Sign up for her newsletter here.
scarlettscottauthor.com/contact
Follow Scarlett on Amazon
Follow Scarlett on BookBub
www.instagram.com/scarlettscottauthor
www.twitter.com/scarscoromance
www.pinterest.com/scarlettscott
www.facebook.com/AuthorScarlettScott
Join the Historical Harlots on Facebook

Manufactured by Amazon.ca
Bolton, ON

39914046R00072